Welcome to the wonderful Romance!
For a free short story and to listen to me read the first chapter of all my other Regencies, please go to my website:

https://romancenovelsbyglrobinson.com

Thank you!

GL Robinson

Cecilia

Or

Too Tall To Love

A Regency Romance
By
GL Robinson

©GL Robinson 2020. All Rights Reserved.

In memory of my dear sister,

Francine.

With thanks to my Beta Readers, and especially to CS for his careful editing and patient technical help.

Cover art: *Juliet* John William Waterhouse 1898

CONTENTS

Chapter One 1
Chapter Two 11
Chapter Three 23
Chapter Four 30
Chapter Five 42
Chapter Six 53
Chapter Seven 66
Chapter Eight 80
Chapter Nine 96
Chapter Ten 108
Chapter Eleven 115
Chapter Twelve 131
Chapter Thirteen 145
Chapter Fourteen 160
Chapter Fifteen 173
Chapter Sixteen 189
Chapter Seventeen 195
Chapter Eighteen 202
THE END 209
A Note From the Author 1
Regency Novels by GL Robinson 2
BOOK GROUP CONVERSATION STARTERS 7

Chapter One

Cecilia Beaumaris sat on her narrow bed and stared out of the window into the garden. It was hard to imagine she would probably never see it all again. She loved its barely controlled wildness, especially since beyond the gates the City of London was growing ever nearer. Here, though, the climbing roses on the side of the building dropped showers of petals on anyone who happened to brush by and grew unchecked into the honeysuckle, so that the flowers of the two shrubs bloomed together in perfect harmony. Against the other end of the wall, the honeysuckle in turn wove its way into the Virginia creeper. Its white and yellow blossoms peeped out from between the green leaves climbing the side of the building, now turning gold at the edges as the summer waned. Asters and marigolds crowded in the flower beds, like young women flaunting their summer bonnets one last time before being forced to put them away for the winter.

For what seemed all her life, she had been at Miss Farridge's Academy for Young Ladies. It was located in the Borough of Holborn, between the commercial center of London known as the City and the residential areas of Mayfair, which might as well have been another country, so rarely had she penetrated its orderly streets. Cecilia's parents, both possessed of an independence that allowed them to do what they chose, had been self-professed scholars and amateur geologists. They spent much of their time in the winter discussing together questions of philosophy, and in the summer descending into caves and tapping at rocks with large hammers. They had found books, fossils, and layers of sedimentary rock more interesting than their young daughter, and she was accustomed to a series of nannies and governesses. These, however, came and went with great regularity. They would be found defective in some way, for, although her parents had no intention of doing it themselves, they had very strict ideas on how a child should be raised. She was to be taught to think for herself: question everything, accept nothing, and believe only what could be demonstrated by scientific evidence. Her mother's favorite question had been, "But how do you *know*?" Most of her childhood preceptresses had been attached to old wives' tales, legends or fairy stories, and they could never answer that all important question. They had had to go.

Unfortunately, this adherence to scientific principles did not prevent Cecilia's parents from tapping with their hammers on the inside of a cave, which gave every evidence, unobserved by them in their enthusiasm, of being subject to rock falls. They brought the roof of the cave down upon themselves. She was left an orphan at ten, a tall, self-sufficient, introspective child with no attachment to anyone. Placed in the care of her father's older brother and his wife, who, with no children of their own, had no more desire to raise a child than her parents had, she was immediately sent to Miss Farridge's establishment. She had remained there ever since.

For the first time in her life, however, she had found there someone who was genuinely interested in her, and who became both a teacher and friend. This was Miss Laura Warren, at the time of Cecilia's arrival, a sensible and warm-hearted woman in her late thirties, who had never married but who was fond of children. She loved Cecilia, seeing in her a lost little girl whose hard carapace hid a tender heart.

Under her kind and encouraging tutelage, Cecilia developed a real love of learning. She understood what her parents had not, that fairy stories and legends, while not based in science, taught lessons that could be learned more pleasurably than listening to a list of explanations. She studied Latin and French with pleasure, becoming quite proficient in both, though neither she nor Miss Warren had ever been nearer to France than a short trip to Worthing, where Miss Warren had a sister. The young ladies of the Academy were also taught to paint, sing, trip a country dance with grace and sew a fine seam, all accomplishments that would stand them in good stead when they sallied forth into the world to find husbands and set up their own establishments.

Most of them found these skills much more to their liking than Molière or Racine or the Odes of Horace. More to their liking still were the novels of Ann Radcliffe and Eliza Parsons which, in principle, were forbidden at the school, but circulated freely nonetheless. Cecilia found these tales ridiculous and more a subject for scorn than spine-tingling horror. And as for the idea of a hero riding on a white horse to rescue the maiden from her dreadful fate, she found it positively ridiculous. She had grown up with nearly no contact with men, and those she had encountered struck her as feeble in the extreme. Her own father had looked much like a woodland animal as he read interminably, crouched over his book, his spectacles low on his nose. Her mother had been the force in the household. Her uncle, in the brief while she had been in his company, had seemed incapable of expressing a coherent thought. He had had difficulty explaining to her that she was to go away to school.

"Yes… er, Cecily (he could not even remember her name correctly). Your aunt and I… er, well… er, don't y' know, better for us... for you, that is, to go away for your education," he had stammered. "A good school will teach you what you need to know and... er, so on. Capital. Capital."

She had thought at the time that since it was clear from her aunt's cold manner she did not want Cecilia there, why did they simply not say so? She had said nothing, just fixed her gold-brown rather piercing gaze on her uncle. He had quailed under her stare and had turned away. Since then, the only men she had come to know at all were old Williams, the gardener, and his assistant Billy, a simple overgrown lad who, while willing to do whatever she asked, was not intellectually or physically prepossessing.

At sixteen, when she had learned all the Academy had to teach her, rather than return home and ultimately be introduced into society like the other girls of her age, she had asked to remain as a teacher. Since one of the older mistresses had just retired, the moment was opportune, and she had stayed. She had been there eight years when her friend and mentor Miss Warren, who had always been subject to a condition of the lungs that sometimes made it almost impossible for her to breathe, had a serious attack. It was feared she would die.

Luckily, swift intervention by a young doctor who was familiar with the disease was able to arrest the symptoms of what he termed *asthma*. He had the teacher breathe in from a bowl filled with hot water and the leaves of a plant called devil's snare. This combination, which had apparently been used from the time of the Romans, calmed Miss Warren's breathing and she was at length deemed out of danger. But he urged her to move away from the dirt of the city and live close to the sea, and above all, not to exert herself making beds, sweeping the floor, or doing any activity where dust might penetrate her lungs. Her sister lived in a quiet way in Worthing, and it was decided she would move there. The milder climate on the other side of the Downs and walks by the sea would help to keep her attacks under control.

Cecilia was devastated at the idea of her friend's leaving and begged that she might go too. But, for once, Miss Warren was adamant.

"No, my dear," she said firmly. "It is not right for you to shut yourself away with two old ladies. You are young still, and in a year, when you are twenty-five, as you know, you will have the management of your fortune. I do not believe it to be princely, but since you have spent nearly none of it these last years, it must be worth a reasonable sum. You are not pretty in the common way, but with your height and your carriage, you are arresting. If you would just pay a little more attention to your dress and your hair, as I have often advised, I know you would be considered a handsome woman. I cannot but believe there is a man somewhere out there who would make you a worthy husband. You love children. Do not make the mistake I did and cut yourself off from the felicity of having your own little ones. There is no finer calling than that of a mother, after all."

Remembering her own mother's almost total disregard for her daughter, Cecilia thought that some might dispute that last statement, but after arguing with her friend for what seemed like days, she had to accept that going to Worthing was not an option.

A further blow came in the shape of Miss Farridge's announcement of the governors' decision to close the school and sell the premises. When it had been established, the school lay in undeveloped land outside the City, but the expansion of commerce had made the value of the premises higher than the fees they might expect to receive, especially with the head teacher leaving.

Miss Warren then took matters into her own hands and wrote to Cecilia's uncle and aunt, explaining the situation. They received a letter almost immediately, inviting Cecilia to make her home with them. They were now at an age when they could see that having a younger person about the place might be useful. The aunt was not warm by nature and took a quick dislike to most people, so had not been able to keep anyone in the way of a companion. Cecilia might fill the post, and the good news was that, since she was family, they would not have to pay her. They did not say this in the letter, of course, but Cecilia was shrewd enough to work it out. She consoled herself with the thought that in just a year she would be master of her own fortune and her own destiny. She would be independent.

Cecilia's emotions at saying goodbye to her old friend were much more intense than when her parents had died. The school had become her home and Miss Warren both mother and friend. But now, for the second time in her life, she had to leave everything she knew and go forth alone, into an unknown future.

It was with a heavy heart that she climbed into the carriage her uncle had sent, the trunk containing her few possessions already having been loaded. With promises of frequent letters, she left for Mayfair. As the carriage wound its way west, the dwellings became grander, the roads cleaner and wider and even the trees looked greener. The discreet flowers growing in the small green patches in front of the houses did not intermingle with their neighbors or flaunt their bonnets. They would not have dared.

Her uncle, Lord Alfred Beaumaris, her father's older brother, had a townhouse on Bruton Street, an address that Cecilia did not recognize as being slightly second rate, but which was one of the causes of his wife's constant discontent. The coachman pulled the front doorbell and then let down the steps for her to dismount.

A stately butler held the door open for her and muttered "Miss Beaumaris, I presume?" She nodded and followed his deliberate steps into a drawing room.

"Miss Beaumaris," he intoned with great solemnity, as she passed in front of him. The eyes of the two persons inside nearly started from their heads as they beheld their niece. She had left them a little girl and now returned, a very tall, stately young woman. She must have been at least five feet nine inches, her figure, as far as they could tell in her round gown of an undistinguished grey, slim though well-formed, her hair, which had been an untamed profusion of curls as a girl, now confined into the nape of her long neck and topped by a bonnet that was more serviceable than modish. She was not pretty or well-dressed but was nevertheless a striking figure.

"My dear niece! Welcome home!" cried her uncle, coming forward and taking her hand. "You remember your aunt Mabel, I'm sure." He led her to his wife, who had not risen from the sofa on which she half sat, half lay.

Cecilia murmured something indistinct and took her aunt's hand, limp and cold as a dead fish.

"Cecily!" said her aunt, with an attempt at enthusiasm. "How nice to have you with us once more."

"My name is Cecilia," pronounced the new arrival clearly. "I remember you did not know it last time, the only time, I was here."

Her aunt and uncle looked at each other in dismay. To say that they were already regretting their generosity in inviting this strange young woman into their home was, perhaps, a little premature, but they both had the distinct feeling that she was not going to be the complaisant fetch-and-carry damsel they had expected.

Her ladyship struggled almost to her feet, "Well, Cecilia, I'm sure you wish to go to your room and remove your bonnet. I would come up with you, but my legs, I'm afraid, are far from steady these days. My housekeeper, Mrs. Browning, will accompany you. Please address yourself to her if you are in need of anything." She collapsed back onto the sofa and signaled to her husband to ring the bell.

Led upstairs by the housekeeper, Cecilia found herself in the same bedroom she had inhabited during her brief stay all those years ago. It had not changed to any great degree. The bed, which had seemed vast and cold to her when she was ten, she now saw was of a normal size, and the rest was the same. The furniture was of a dark mahogany that looked as if it had been there forever, which, indeed, it had. It had been bought with the house and dated from just before Charles II had returned to the capital; it was ponderous and gloomy. But Cecilia had not grown up surrounded by beautiful things, so it did not bother her.

While she was taking off her bonnet and washing her hands in the cold water provided by the jug and basin on her washstand, her trunk arrived, carried by a footman at one end and, to judge from the blue-grey apron that enveloped most of her small body, a scullery maid at the other. The footman bowed and departed, leaving Cecilia wondering if she should have given him a *douceur*, but the maid remained and, having undone the straps of the trunk, made to unpack it.

"Oh, I can do it myself," said Cecilia quickly. "There isn't much, anyway."

"If you please, Miss, I'm s'pposed to 'elp. The upstairs maids is all busy, so they sent me. P'haps if you pass me the things I can 'ang them up. Please, Miss."

"Oh, very well, if you like!" agreed Cecilia.

They quickly put away her few gowns and underclothes, and the maid, whose name turned out to be Bridget, was amazed to see that the bottom half of Cecilia's trunk was full of books.

"'Ave you read 'em all, Miss?" she asked in amazement.

"Yes, but I like to look at them again and again, I never tire of my books."

Bridget had picked up one of the books of stories illustrated with line drawings that Cecilia had used to teach the younger girls at the school. She found that if they could match words with pictures, they made quicker progress.

"What's this one about then? I wish I could read. I never learned proper," said the maid, looking at the story about Dick Whittington and his cat.

"Look at the picture. What do you think?"

"A man and 'is cat?"

"That's right. Look, there's the word for *cat* and the man's name is *Dick*." Cecilia showed her the two words, which she then picked out every time they appeared on the next couple of pages. "Why didn't you learn to read? Didn't you go to school?"

"Sometimes I did, but I 'ad to 'elp me mum with all the little 'uns and the washin' an' all. The boys went, though. Me bruvvers can all read 'n write," she ended proudly.

"Don't you have to be able to read and write to work in a big house like this?"

"Not if you works in the scullery or washroom, or carryin' up the coal. You 'ave to if you wants to be an upstairs maid or lady's maid, a'course. But there's not many jobs. I was lucky to get a place 'ere. One of me bruvvers walks out wiv the cook's 'elper, Amy 'er name is. An' she got me the job."

"Well, Bridget, come and see me whenever you can, and I'll teach you. You can take the book if you like. Bring it back when you come. See if you can find *cat* or *Dick* anywhere else." As the maid gasped in pleasure and clasped the book to her thin bosom, Cecilia suddenly asked, "But before you go, tell me, what happens to girls like yourself who cannot read or write, and no brother to help them get a job?"

"Well, Miss," answered the maid, looking at the floor, "they tries to get work anywhere they can, in the fact'ries, fr'instance, but if not, they 'as to do what they can. They may 'ave to… you know, not be any better'n they should be."

"You mean, go into prostitution?" Then, thinking that perhaps Bridge might not understand the word, "Sell themselves… to men?"

"Yes, Miss," whispered Bridget. "That's what I mean."

At that moment, Cecilia knew what she was going to do with her life.

Chapter Two

Downstairs, Lord and Lady Beaumaris were having an urgent, low-voiced conversation.

"Oh, my dear! She won't do at all!" exclaimed the lady, *sotto voce*. "She's far too tall! I declare I'll get a crick in my neck looking up at her all the time. And she doesn't seem especially ... *biddable.* That nonsense about her name, and the direct way she looks at one. Why. I'm almost *afraid* of her! No, no!"

"She's a Long Meg, and no mistake," replied her husband thoughtfully. "But not bad looking, for all that. There's something about her ..." He pondered a moment. "I know! We'll put it about she's got a fortune. She does have some money; I don't know how much. M'brother left all that in the hands of his man of business, but the idea's enough to bring the fellers sniffing around. Bound to be someone there who'll have her, for all she's too tall and not a spring chicken. What is she? Twenty-four? Yes, let's get her married and she'll be off our hands. Tell you what, you have a couple of tea parties. Introduce her to all the old biddies and let it slip she's an heiress. Be vague about it. I'll wager the word will get out. She'll be invited everywhere and if she don't have an offer in under three months, I'll be astonished."

"Tea parties?" echoed his lady weakly. I don't know. With the state of my health ..."

"Oh, tush, tush! Mrs. Browning will see to it all, have no fear. You just give the girl the word that she's got to put on her party manners. No staring at people in that awkward way she has.

Look, you said yourself she's no good here. Marrying her off is the only answer. You'll see."

So it was that Cecilia found herself over the next month sitting down to tea with a variety of society dames whose names she was hard put to remember once the afternoon was over. When cards bearing their names began to appear with invitations to dinners, loo-parties, musical soirées, and, daringly, a starlit *al fresco* ridotto (perhaps a trifle too late in the season, but September had so far been very warm), she never knew which face to put with which hostess until she was greeted at the top of the stairs.

She heard the word *heiress* muttered around the rooms but never supposed it referred to her. She was not to know that her lack of a modish wardrobe and plain way of presenting herself, which had at first surprised those who thought her well-heeled, had been explained away by her aunt as the result of having lived in seclusion with an ancient relative until very recently. But then the offers of marriage began. She would be introduced to a gentleman. He would pay her the sort of attention that to those familiar with the marriage mart would have been obvious, but to her, unaccustomed as she was to society of this sort, was merely friendly. The next couple of times they were in the same place, he would attach himself to her side again, and then, very shortly afterwards, present himself in Bruton Street with a declaration of affection, though never love, and an offer of marriage.

The first time it happened, she was as embarrassed as she was astonished, for she had never given the gentleman any indication of partiality and could not imagine why he should want to marry her. After the third such proposal, she finally asked the suitor point blank why he was thus offering himself to her. He had answered more truthfully than he would have done, had he been given time to think,

"Well, I can see you haven't much town bronze, but I've been on the town for an age. You're a wealthy woman and I ... I could help you to establish yourself in society. I know what's what, I assure you. Besides, you're a ... a good-looking woman – need a new gown or two, of course – and I think we could deal famously together. Come on, Cecily, say you will!"

"Thank you for your frankness," she had replied calmly. "I wish I could reward it by saying I will accept your ... your generous offer, but I'm afraid I cannot. I have no intention of marrying you, or anyone else. And if I may give you a hint: when you next propose to a woman, make sure you know her name. Mine is Cecilia, not Cecily."

Not unnaturally, the confused suitor made his escape as quickly as he could, leaving Miss Beaumaris with much to think about. At length, she went looking for her uncle and finally ran him to ground in the wine room where he was tasting the first bottle from several cases laid down by his father some fifty years before. One look at her determined countenance caused her uncle to dismiss the butler and seek a protective chair to stand behind.

"Uncle," she said without preamble, "have you or my aunt been telling people that I'm an heiress?"

"An heiress, my dear? N... no, not an heiress. We may have let slip that you have a genteel fortune. I'm not sure what you have, to tell you the truth, my brother did not see fit to leave me in charge of your financial affairs. But we thought it best," he added quickly, "for a pretty girl with a fortune is more attractive than one without."

"But I am not a pretty girl and, as far as I know, I have nothing approaching a fortune. But in any case, I should tell you, uncle, I have no thought of marriage. I have today refused the third suitor to my hand and I shall continue to refuse as many as may feel it necessary to address me. Next year, when I am twenty-five and may manage my own affairs, I shall move out to live with some sort of useful chaperone, not in such an elegant locality as this, but somewhere in a less genteel neighborhood, where I shall open a school for impoverished girls. I promise you, after my next birthday I shall be no further charge on you at all."

She turned on her heel and left her uncle open-mouthed, the glass in his hand tilting more and more precariously towards the floor.

Lord Beaumaris reported this astonishing conversation to his wife, who groaned when she heard that Cecilia had no intention to marry, but brightened when she heard that in under a year, she would be leaving them in any case.

"But opening a school for impoverished girls! What a peculiar idea!" she said. "What can she hope to gain by it? She'll never meet a husband that way. Mark my words, she'll consume her fortune, whatever it may be, and then come running back to us."

"Perhaps, my dear, but hopefully not for many years. She isn't an expensive woman, I'll say that for her. I don't think she's bought a new gown since she's been here. And this idea of educating the poor seems all the crack. That man from Portsmouth is doing it, what was his name? Pounds! That was it. There was an article in the newspaper about it just the other day. He's a cobbler. Has a crowd of them in his workshop every day. Gives 'em baked potatoes to make 'em come to school! Sounds like a rum 'un!"

"Well, I'm sure it's all very worthy and good. I just hope she doesn't bring any of them here and start giving them baked potatoes. My nerves won't stand it."

"No, no, she's going to open a school of her own when she gets her hands on her money. In the meantime, don't say anything to her about getting married, and don't tell any of the biddies she ain't ever going to. Just keep on making sure she's invited. It'll be shooting season soon and people are bound to have weekend parties. Wouldn't mind a bit of sport myself, come to that."

So Cecilia was surprised, when she came down for dinner that night, that the question of marriage was only briefly referred to.

"Did I hear Henry Taverner here this morning, my dear?" her ladyship asked Cecilia neutrally.

"Yes, he came to ask me to marry him," replied the young woman. "I said no and he left. But he did tell me why he offered for me. It's because I'm an heiress, it seems."

"Goodness!" replied her aunt, "That's gossip for you. One only has to mention that a girl has a genteel competence for it to become a fortune overnight. I hope you put him right!"

"Yes, and I told him that the next time he offers for someone, he'd better get her name right. He called me Cecily. It's funny how people often do, I wonder why."

She knew perfectly well why: both her aunt and uncle persisted in this error, though they certainly should have known better by now. Nothing more was said on the subject.

Her uncle, however, in an attempt, perhaps, to make up for his constant mistake with her name, mentioned the *Times* article about John Pounds and said he would look it out for her. This interested her much more than the talk about marriage. She thought she would write to Mr. Pounds for advice. She did not say this, but led the conversation onto the question of education in general, and they had a more convivial dinner than they had hitherto enjoyed.

It became clear, however, that her ladyship herself had scarcely ever read a book. As a young woman she had been taught that novels were deleterious to a girl's morals and had consequently read none. But since she did not like anything else, she had simply not read at all. When she considered how little use her aunt had made of the education she had received, compared with Bridget who was overjoyed at the chance of learning to read, she felt that the decision she had made about her future was the right one.

For Bridget had taken Cecilia at her word and whenever she could, stole up to her room for a lesson, no matter how brief. Cecilia had taught her the alphabet and the sounds of the letters.

"I told Mrs. Browning you'd asked for me partic'lar, cos you needs something moving. But I prob'ly can't stay more than 'alf an hour." She had said earlier that afternoon. "But look Miss, I've put all the words I've learned next to the letter they begins with."

Cecilia had written out the alphabet down the left side of the front and back of a piece of paper. She now saw that Bridget had drawn a line across the page underneath each letter and had written the words she now recognized on the appropriate line.

"You are writing a dictionary, Bridget!" said Cecilia, impressed by the work the girl had done.

"What's a diction'ry, Miss?"

"A list of all the words in a language, with what they mean. Look!" she went to her books, arranged along the back of a table against the wall. "This is Dr. Johnson's *Dictionary of the English Language*. If we look in here, we shall find the word *cat*, with an explanation of what it means."

She quickly found the entry and read:

A domestick animal that catches mice, commonly reckoned by naturalists the lowest order of the leonine species.

"What's d'mestik, Miss?"

"It means *belonging to a house or home*."

"And what's leenine?"

"Leonine. It means *like a lion*."

"I ain't never seen a lion, Miss."

"Well, it truly does look like a very big cat."

"So the cat is like a little lion living in a 'ouse?" Bridget turned over the leaves of the dictionary with wonder. "This Dr. Johnson must 'ave been ever so clever. "E knew what everything meant."

"Yes, but when he was a little boy he had to learn to read, just like you, and I daresay you are as good at it as he was. You have made your own dictionary, after all. Bridget's Dictionary."

"Bridget's Diction'ry. Won't me mum be proud when she see what I done?"

"I'm sure she will, but we still have to learn lots more words and write them down. You will need more paper. I shall get some tomorrow."

"It's not so much the paper, Miss, it's the time to do it. I've been writin' at night after I goes to bed, but now it's getting darker, I won't be able to cos we've only got the one candle for the week, me and the other two girls in the room, and if I keeps it burnin', it won't last."

"I think it may be time to take Mrs. Browning into our confidence." Then, seeing the maid's puzzled expression, "Tell her what we're doing. I can buy more paper and candles, but I think it's best to tell her why."

"But she won't stop me learnin' to read, will she, Miss?"

"No. I'll make sure of that."

The next day, Cecilia explained to the housekeeper that she was teaching Bridget to read and write.

"I'm persuaded, she said, "that a woman of your sense and abilities will see what a good thing it is for all girls to learn these essential skills. She will not shirk her other duties, I promise you."

Mrs. Browning hesitated at first, but then agreed that, provided the girl's work was done, she was free to learn in her own time.

"In fact, Miss, I will suggest that she work at the kitchen table for an hour every night after everything is cleared away. That way, she will not keep the other girls from sleep and not use unnecessary candles. We have oil lamps in the kitchen and one is always left burning low in case anything is needed in the night. She can turn it down when she goes to bed."

Thereafter, whenever Cecilia was at home in the evenings, she went down to the kitchens and gave Bridget her lessons. Her uncle usually went to his club and her aunt was rather afraid of her niece and her direct questions, so was glad not to have to sit with her. It wasn't too long before, going down to the kitchen, she saw Bridget leaning over another girl with the Dick Whittington story open in front of them, teaching her *cat* and *Dick,* just as she had been taught herself. Her heart rose. This was going to work!

In the meantime, the invitations continued to come in, and so too did more offers of marriage, though she told her suitors she had no fortune to speak of. Ironically, this only encouraged the more persistent amongst them, since they thought she was merely being coy. Some of the older mamas remembered her mother and father, who certainly lived well, if unconventionally. Cecilia herself had never given her parents' fortune, or lack of it, much thought.

She had been paid enough by Miss Farridge's establishment to more than cover her modest needs. She spent more on books than anything else. She had lived at the school, where she also received her meals, so she had been able to save a small sum. This she now used for paper, pencils and candles for her pupils, and the odd necessary item for herself. She thought that when she ran out of money, she would address herself to Mr. William Davis in the City. This gentleman had written to her punctiliously once a year since she was ten, assuring her of his continued attention to her affairs, but she had never responded. In fact, she had never met him.

One morning at breakfast her aunt slit open a letter with her ivory opener, and having perused it declared delightedly, "How nice! Lady March invites us all the weekend after next to

Highmount for the shooting. It will be the first shooting party of the season. I imagine all the best people will be there." A thought suddenly struck her. "You do have a garment or two suitable for the country, I hope, Cecilia?"

"Why? Does one wear different clothes there than at home?"

"Of, course! If one is to join the gentlemen for lunch in the field, one needs good wool outfits and boots. It can be quite muddy, though, of course, we shall not be expected to walk through the fields. A gig will take us, no doubt. One does not wear silks during the day in the country."

Cecilia ran through her wardrobe in her mind. She only had her old wool dress from her days teaching in the chilly classrooms of Mrs. Farridge's establishment and it was sadly worn. Boots were not a problem, as she had been accustomed to walking a great deal before coming to Bruton Street.

"And, of course, one needs a pretty gown for the evening. Or two really."

"I think I shall have to stay here, aunt," said Cecilia regretfully. She would have liked a day or two in the country. Shooting certainly did not interest her, but the countryside would undoubtedly be lovely in early October. "I have nothing at all of what you describe. The evening gowns I have would probably do for dinner, but …."

This did not suit her aunt, who was still thinking of possible suitors to Cecilia's hand, and also looking forward to a weekend with Lady March. They always did one very well at Highmount. She thought quickly.

"I have a couple of country costumes that no longer… no longer become me." What she meant was, that they no longer fit her, as her sedentary lifestyle had resulted in an increased girth. "I think they could be made up for you. They will be much too short, of course, but we shall see."

After breakfast, she bore her niece upstairs where she ordered her dresser to find the old wool costumes she was sure were in the back of her wardrobe. They were finally produced, and proved to be voluminous garments from the previous century, with gathered skirts and separate jackets fitted to the waist, with a peplum. Unfortunately, the moth had attacked two of the garments, a fact which caused Lady Beaumaris to roundly criticize her dresser for not brushing them regularly, but one of them, in a bottle green wool, had remained untouched. Since the color was the one that became Cecilia the best, this was considered a godsend.

With some misgivings, Cecilia removed her gown and stood in her petticoat as the dresser slipped the wide skirt over her head and drew it in around her waist. As predicted, it was far too short, but it was also far too wide, so it was clear a panel or two could be removed from the width to attach to the bottom. The waisted bodice fit surprisingly well across the bosom, for Lady Beaumaris was plump in that area, but was too short and narrow in the shoulders.

"Perhaps we could simply remove the sleeves and the peplum and I could wear it as a waistcoat with a blouse underneath. It won't matter then if it's a bit short." suggested Cecilia. "I can keep a shawl around my shoulders indoors and wear my cloak outside. I believe I am already regarded as somewhat unconventional, so it should shock no one."

Her aunt and her dresser looked a little doubtful, but finally agreed that this had the advantage of being a fairly simple alteration which could be accomplished between the dresser and Mrs. Browning.

In the end, the result was not to be despised. Once the skirt was reduced in volume, it suited Cecilia's slim hips and narrow waist, and the housekeeper had the brainwave of covering the seam that went around the skirt to lengthen it with a piece of black binding. This had been left over from trimming hats during a period of mourning some years previously, and was also used to hem the cut edges of the bodice. In the end, the outfit had a slightly military look, which the ladies all thought quite the thing in view of the recent engagements on the Continent.

Cecilia found herself more in charity with her aunt than she had ever been before, especially when that lady, in a fit of generosity that surprised even herself, gave her niece a lovely silk shawl to wear with her overused and drab evening gowns. It was embroidered in gold and chestnut brown, which suited Cecilia's eyes and complexion admirably, whereas it overwhelmed the faded blond hair and pale blue eyes of her aunt.

So it was with a pleasant sense of anticipation that Miss Beaumaris set out in the carriage with her aunt and uncle for a weekend in the country. She had left Bridget work to do, she had written to Mr. Pounds for advice on opening a school and she was quite looking forward to wearing her new outfit. She had even purchased a new curling feather for her old bonnet. It was a golden brown, just like her eyes, and while she told herself she could have no pretensions to beauty, she knew herself to look as well as could be expected of a too-tall woman no longer very young, of a decidedly blue-stocking disposition and with no wardrobe to speak of.

Chapter Three

"Where on earth have you been this age, Tommy?" said the Dowager Lady Ianthe Broome wearing a very becoming lace cap and a layer of paint on her face so subtle that only her dresser knew for certain it was there. "I've sent messages to Broome House I don't know how many times these last few weeks and you have responded to none of them. And for mercy's sake, stop looking at yourself in the mirror!"

"I'm sorry, Grandmother," said Thomas George Augustus Allenby, fourth Earl of Broome, his eyes twinkling at her, "but every time I catch a reflection of myself, I am convinced that Weston made the tails of this coat a trifle too long. Brummel always said it was his linings that let him down, but I find the lining irreproachable."

He turned himself this way and that in front of the tall pier mirror hanging in the pretty parlor where he was now being scolded by the matriarch of the Broome family. "But the length in the back, that is altogether another matter." He considered his reflection thoughtfully before continuing, "Anyway, I've been down at Thyford, seein' to business. The harvest. Someone has to, you know." He stood before her, a good-looking man in his mid-thirties, a little above average height, and of a perfection of physique that was a gratification to his tailor and the joy of his valet.

"I don't see why,' retorted his grandmother. "In my day we had agents and bailiffs to look after the estates. I can't imagine you can do much good there in any case. The only thing you seem to care about is the cut of your coats!"

"How can you say that, Granny, when you know I care every bit as much about my boots!" He grinned at her.

His grandmother was in no way mollified by the use of the pet name he had used for her when he was a boy. She rapped the tip of her cane smartly on the parquet floor. "For heaven's sake, be serious and pay attention, Tommy, before I become truly vexed with you! Your coat is perfectly fine. At least, the length is perfectly fine. Whether the stripe or the daffodil lining are fine, no doubt you are the best judge of that. In my day, no man would be seen wearing such a thing!"

"But Grandmother," remonstrated the Earl, coming to her with a charming smile and going to a footstool next to her low chair, "how can you say that with a straight face when you know my revered grandfather, may he rest in peace, wore a pink silk coat trimmed with acres of lace, over a gold waistcoat embroidered all over with mirrors. I was looking at the portrait of him in the gallery at Thyford in just such a rig-out only the other day. I am nothing to him!"

"That is very true, for he knew what was due to his family," replied the old lady, tartly. "He married where his parents directed him and even though we had barely set eyes on each other before our betrothal, between us we managed to ensure the family line. We produced your father and his brother, not to mention your poor aunt Martha who married that *dreadful* man."

The Earl's aunt Martha had made the mistake of marrying for love a man who was of a lower social order than she. He was a mill owner in Manchester and actually very well-off, but this never prevented her mother from referring to her daughter as *poor*.

"It was not our fault if your uncle Peregrine decided to go over to the colony in America and fight in that stupid war. Much good it did any of us! We lost a son and England lost the colony. I know George hasn't been himself for some time, but letting those rebels get away with it! I wonder he can hold his head up at the Palace!"

"Well, he doesn't hold his head up, the Prince Regent does it for him, or instead of him, I should say. Now there's a man whose tailor makes him! Last time I saw him he was the size of at least two men, but his tailor disguised it admirably. The cut of his coat was something to behold."

His grandmother rapped her cane again. "Tommy! Keep your mind on the matter at hand! Forget the Prince's tailor, and your own, and apply yourself to the problem. With your father and mother both drowning during that trip to Switzerland, and you their only son, we have to think about the succession. What gave them the idea that sailing across the lake on a stormy day could possibly have a satisfactory outcome, I cannot imagine. But the fact is, it's now up to you to ensure there's an heir. God help us!"

"It wasn't stormy when they set out, Grandmother. You can't blame them for the weather!"

"I do blame them, not for dying, which anyone may do, but for not providing the family with another son to ensure the birth of an heir, since you appear to have no intention of doing so."

"But Grandmother!" protested the Earl. "You can't blame them for that either! It's not as if they didn't try. I have two sisters. They did their best!"

"Two sisters! Bah! Much good they are! You know as well as I do that no son of theirs, if they manage to produce any, may succeed to the Earldom of Broome."

"Indeed, you are too harsh. They are both very pretty girls and have made good marriages. And while they may not provide an heir, they are of little or no call on the finances of the estate, you know."

"I know no such thing, nor care to know. The finances are none of my concern."

His lordship reflected ruefully that this was true. His grandmother had no sense of fiscal responsibility whatsoever. She had always been amazingly expensive. He remembered his father clutching his head in agony as he tried to make sense of the mass of bills she regularly thrust into his hands, in spite of the fact that she was supposed to live within the limits of her own, not inconsiderable, fortune.

She absolutely refused to live in the Dower House at Thyford, and insisted on running her house in London, bought thirty-five years earlier at enormous expense, as if a family of at least twelve were living there, rather than a dowager countess alone. She insisted on fires in all the rooms most of the year, burned a king's ransom of wax candles even in the kitchen, every three years threw out her household effects, including all the linens, furniture and draperies, and replaced it all with brand new items, imported most often from Paris, until the recent troubles had made this impossible. If she deplored the rampage of Bonaparte across Europe, it was not because the flower of English manhood was cut down trying to prevent it, but because it prevented her from ordering her bed linen from a certain establishment in the Rue St. Honoré.

As for her gowns, though she regularly criticized Tommy roundly for his sartorial excesses, she spent every bit as much as he did on her raiment without ever considering for a moment from whom he might have inherited this tendency.

She called him to order again. "You are the most infuriating creature, Thomas! I am trying to talk to you about marriage and you keep turning the subject. Now pay attention!"

When she called him Thomas, he knew he had to buckle under. There was no escaping the natural force that was his paternal grandmother. He sighed and rose from the footstool, going to an armchair as far from the fire as he could and still be in his grandmother's line of vision. He adopted the expression of a man prepared to listen to unwelcome intelligence. It was not long in coming.

"I have arranged with my old friend Lady March for you to join them at a party this weekend at Highmount. It's the first shooting party of the season. She tells me that the Beaumaris girl will be there. She's appeared on the scene while you've been away. I haven't met her personally as I don't go out much these days."

This was true. The dowager sat in her living room and the world, in the shape of the older generation of the *ton*, came to her. There was no one better informed of the *on-dits* than she.

"She's not in the common way, apparently, not flighty like most of them these days. I'm told she has a fortune, but no one seems to know the details. Not that you need the money, since you inherited enough to buy an abbey, as the saying goes, without mentioning what you will get from me when the time comes, but," and here she unconsciously echoed the words of

Cecilia's uncle, "a nice-looking girl with a fortune is always better than a nice-looking girl without."

"Oh, no, Gran!" he groaned. "Not another one! Every time you find a new wife for me, she's worse than the last! How many shrill-voiced, clinging damsels are left in the world for me to meet? The last one presented herself to me wearing a pink gown! *Pink*! I ask you, and she had hair the color of dandelions in the spring." He shuddered visibly. No, I simply cannot do it, not even for a fortune, no matter how much it may be!"

"Do not call me that, Thomas! You know I dislike it intensely." replied his grandmother, with spirit. "Indeed, you are too nice! Miss Williams is considered very good-looking by men with more discernment than you *and* she has fifty thousand a year. But it's too late now, you've lost your chance. I hear she's accepted Henry Taverner."

"Since the last time I saw him he was wearing a waistcoat that looked as if it had been cut from a circus tent, I have no doubt they will deal exceedingly well together. But if he discerned much more than the fifty thousand, it would surprise me. I hear he's towed so far up the River Tick his boat may disappear from view."

"Do not use that language with me, Thomas, we are not in some low tavern, that I make no doubt you frequent. But take careful note of what I say. You will meet Miss Beaumaris and unless she is a positive antidote, which is unlikely, or Elizabeth March would have told me, you will make her an offer. Do not come back to me without a betrothal in your pocket."

The Earl stood up and walked over to his granddame. "I have always loved you, Grandmother, more than any of my relatives," he said formally, but with a smile in his eyes. "But I fear we are never to meet again. You must know, for I am more like you than anyone in the family, that I shall never marry simply to please you and that nothing will induce me to offer for a young woman anything like those you have caused to be thrown in my path these last three years. I shall go to Highmount, as the shooting there is always more than fair, but if the only way we can meet after this weekend is if I have a betrothal in my pocket, then this is goodbye forever."

His bow was a model of perfection and his kiss on her fingertips a wonderful combination of affection and dismissal. As he walked to the door, he caught a glimpse of himself in the tall mirror.

"I still say the tails of this coat are a fraction too long. And perhaps you are right about the daffodil. I shall have to give it some very serious thought."

"Ridiculous boy!" said his grandmother fondly, as he disappeared. And she sighed.

Chapter Four

To avoid meeting the young woman his grandmother had chosen for him, or any of the others he had let down as kindly as he could, Tommy Allenby arrived at Highmount as late as he dared. He judged that by the time he changed and went down, they would be called almost immediately to table. After dinner he would take refuge in the billiard room and avoid the ladies altogether. Tomorrow they would not appear for breakfast and, with the shooting beginning afterwards, he would be safe until the evening. If he could, he would repeat the performance tomorrow, appear at the last minute before dinner and escape afterwards. He was aware that this was hardly fair to his hostess and hoped she had not planned any dancing which he would not be able, with propriety, to avoid. But he knew his credit with her was good and hoped that his behavior would not be reported back to his grandmother.

He had scarcely two hours to scramble into his evening clothes before dinner, a length of time he considered only just sufficient. He counted it as a credit to his calm temperament that in under an hour he was able to bathe, pull on his tight white satin knee britches and silk stockings, the linen shirt with the highly starched collar points, and his silk waistcoat. This allowed another hour for him to arrange the perfection that was his cravat and the careful disorder of his golden curls. His valet then helped him into a coat so closely fitted to his shoulders that at one point it seemed as if he might need two men to get it on. He thanked God that no boots were worn for dinner, since he would have needed another half an hour to put on his Hessians.

The coat he was wearing was not the one that had so disturbed him the week before at his grandmother's. He had hung that one in his closet, or rather, his valet had, with the idea that he would try to forget it. Then, when he came upon it at some later date, he might be able to decide, with a fresh eye, whether an eighth of an inch needed to be taken off the tails, and whether, indeed, the daffodil yellow had been as felicitous a choice as he had at the time believed. The coat he now wore was of a heavy dark green silk, shot through with the faintest hint of gold, the same gold appearing in the lining of the coat and in the paisley pattern of his waistcoat.

He stepped over the pile of crumpled starched neckcloths that lay on the floor, discarded in his first attempts at a complicated fold he thought he might name Tommy's Folly, so difficult was it to achieve. He looked at his reflection one last time. Not the least criticism he had of the infamous daffodil-lined garment was that it had caused him to look at himself several times in his grandmother's mirror. It was Brummel's maxim that a gentleman, having dressed with careful attention to every detail of his appearance, should never look at himself once he left his bedchamber. This was a maxim the Earl took very much to heart. His behavior during his visit to his grandmother had been an aberration, and he could only excuse it to himself by the knowledge that it was the belated receipt of her many peremptory notes that had caused him to rush and leave the house before he was perfectly sure of his appearance. With the knowledge that tonight, however, he had achieved perfection, he went down to dinner.

Cecilia saw him come into the drawing room. She had hidden herself in a corner behind a potted palm, having caught a glimpse of a gentleman who had been pursuing her on the last two occasions they met.

Her first reaction was to laugh and say under her breath, "Good heavens! What a dandy!" Her second was, "But what a handsome one!"

From the top of his golden waves to the tip of his shining shoes he was a veritable picture. She saw him execute an elegant bow to his hostess and kiss her fingertips with grace, before being greeted with pleasure by everyone else. She wondered why she had never seen him before, since he seemed so well known. A pretty young woman came swiftly to his side and looked earnestly up at him, placing her hand on his arm. He smiled charmingly down at her, spoke a few words and moved on.

A few minutes later, the company went into dinner. Cecilia was seated far from the new arrival, whom she promptly ceased to think about, but, unfortunately, next to the gentleman she had been avoiding. Their hostess must have thought she was being kind in her matchmaking, but for Cecilia, it was an ordeal. She tried to converse lightly with both him and the gentleman on her other side, but her suitor looked at her intently, touched her hand meaningfully and, as she left with the other ladies said, "I hope to have a few moments alone with you later, Miss Beaumaris."

Knowing she was about to be importuned with another proposal, when the ladies retired into the drawing room, Cecilia exchanged a few words with Lady March and her aunt, before going to one of the French windows and slipping out into the garden.

It was a lovely night. The moon was full, golden and so low that she felt she might almost touch it. She stepped lightly down the steps on one side of the parterre and walked into the shadow of the trees that lined the wide gravel coach path. Looking back, she could see the figures in the drawing room, lit by the enormous branched chandeliers, moving as if in some sort of pantomime. The silks of the ladies' evening dresses came together and parted as they moved around the room, joining now here, now there.

In a few minutes, the gentlemen arrived, and the silk dresses coupled with the more somber costumes of the men. The green-coated beau was not amongst them. She saw her suitor looking around the room, then go questioningly to her aunt, who shook her head and looked around as well. She had been missed. Fearful he might guess she had come outside, she walked quickly towards the end of the row of trees and around the side of the house.

She passed what was obviously the library, where a low fire burned and a single chandelier provided a minimum of light. Evidently it was not used at this time of night. Next, she came to a much brighter lit room where she quickly saw the green coat of the dandy. He was laughing with a group of other men standing by. The gentlemen reached in their pockets and drew out billfolds, placing banknotes on the side of the billiard table. She watched the dandy take a cue from the rack, survey the table for a moment, then gracefully bend over it, move his cue back and quickly forward.

She could not see what happened, but the other men raised their hands and shook their heads with every evidence of amazement. The dandy just laughed, placed his cue in the rack and picked up the banknotes. The same process was repeated with other men taking turns and winning or losing, their friends reacting with disbelieving acclaim or obvious chaffing. She envied them their easy camaraderie, something she had never herself experienced. She had always been an outsider, she thought. Too tall, too forthright, not interested in what the other young women at school had found so fascinating: romance, love and marriage.

Then a brief gust of wind made her shiver. She drew the embroidered scarf more tightly around her shoulders and turned away from the scene. Continuing swiftly around the side of the house, she found a door that was unlocked and slipped inside. It took her a moment or two to get her bearings, but then she made her way to the grand staircase that rose from the front hall. There was no one about, so she ran lightly up the stairs and into her bedchamber.

Tommy pursued his plan and spent the evening in the billiard room, only emerging at eleven, when, from experience, he knew the tea tray would be brought in and the company would retire for the night.

"Where have you been, you naughty boy?" his hostess asked, not really expecting an answer. She still saw him as the lad she had known when his grandmother brought him with her to Highmount during his Eton days.

"Reading scripture in the library, of course, ma'am," he answered with a laugh in his eyes.

"Don't try to gammon me, you wretch! I know perfectly well you've been in the billiard room playing silly games with the others. Poole told me you were there."

"I must remember to thank Poole for keeping us under such careful watch!" replied Tommy with an ironic smile. "But you shouldn't keep the best brandy in there, if you don't want us taking advantage of it, you know."

He bowed and kissed her hand. "Don't, I beg you, tell my grandmother of my transgression. She sent me here to pay court to some young woman – what was the name? Beaumaris. Where is she? I'd better at least see what she looks like, but don't for God's sake present me. Not tonight. It might give me nightmares."

Lady March looked around the room, then shook her head. "She doesn't appear to be here. In any case, I understand Miles Rowntree is sniffing around her. Perhaps he's popping the question at this very moment. Oh, no! There he is! Talking to Pamela Smith. Wasn't she making eyes at you earlier?"

"Is that what it was? I confess, the shrillness of her voice quite filled my head and rendered me incapable of seeing her eyes. Miles Rowntree can have her. He can have both of them!"

"Be that as it may, if you don't appear after dinner tomorrow, you may be sure I shall inform your grandmother." And, as he tried to remonstrate, she tapped him smartly on the arm with her fan and said, "No, don't look at me like that. I may be the only female here impervious to your charms. I didn't invite you here to play billiards all evening. In fact, I may tell Poole to lock the billiard room door and take away the key."

Tommy looked fretfully at his sleeve where the fan had come into contact with it. "Ma'am, I implore you, have a care to my coat! And lock the billiard room door? Where is your heart? What about the brandy? If I am to converse with all the young women my grandmother wishes me to marry, I shall need a good deal of fortification!"

His hostess was of one mind with his grandmother. "Ridiculous boy!" she said.

Luckily for him, the tea tray was brought in almost immediately and he was able to bow his way out of the room.

As his valet eased him out of his coat, he said anxiously, "I only hope the sleeve has not been damaged by Lady March and her damned fan! I tell you, Brooke, fans are the very devil! When they're not using them to hide behind, though I wish more would hide behind them, women will always be tapping or poking you with them. It's not to be tolerated!"

"I understand, sir," said his patient valet, who bore with his foibles because no one in London looked better in a coat than Lord Broome and because he was, after all, a kind and generous employer, "in the last century, it was quite common for gentlemen of the *ton* to carry fans. Many of them had a fan to match every coat."

"I do believe you're right. Damme if there isn't a portrait of my blessed grandfather with a fan in the gallery at Thyford. What a top of the tulips he was! And yet my grandmother has the temerity to accuse me of being over-nice in my dress. Women are a trial, to be sure! She is forever on at me to get married, and Pamela Smith accused me earlier of abandoning her because I had to spend a few weeks at Thyford. And that's a woman I've spoken to only a few times and danced with twice! Does it mean that if I were married, I should have to stay constantly by my wife's side or be accused of abandonment? It doesn't bear thinking about! There seems to be no pleasing them, at any age. Tell me, Brooke, what do you think of marriage?"

"Well, sir, for myself, I don't think of it at all. The life of a gentleman's gentleman is quite complicated enough without that! But for you, my lord, there is the question of the succession, which I'm sure you don't need reminding of." Tommy groaned. "Quite so, sir. But otherwise, I can only think that a lady always brings a deal of change into a household. One's habits must always be upset, and one's tranquility is at an end. Or so it seems to me."

"And to me!" agreed Tommy, with a sigh.

The following morning went according to plan. He breakfasted with the other gentlemen and rode out to the shooting stands in the gigs provided for the purpose. He wore a belted, double-breasted wool shooting jacket in grey with a blue line check that reflected the bright blue of his eyes, the leather patch where the gun would rest against his shoulder also in grey. While very obviously a shooting jacket, it lay without a wrinkle across shoulders which were surprisingly broad for one of an otherwise slim build, and the belted waist fit him perfectly. It had wide pockets below the belt, in principle for carrying cartridges, but Tommy hated having the shape of his jacket pulled down by their weight, so rarely carried anything more than a handkerchief. The pockets therefore lay straight and tidy against his body. His loader carried all the cartridges. He had black breeks and, over wool stockings, tall black boots waxed against damp but polished to a mirror shine.

The morning was cool; the early October sun, which promised to be warm, had not yet burned through the mist that lay over the earth, so the gentlemen were all swathed in greatcoats that would be removed once the shooting began. The gigs drove them through a wood of tall beech trees, their golden heads in the sun and the leaves at their feet all but invisible beneath the mist. They were let down in an area of open heath with almost waist-high shrubs and they walked to the stands.

It was a fine sight: the men and their loaders, the air faintly perfumed with the sharp scent of gun oil, the dogs' tails visible above the bushes, walking almost in silence. They stood behind the numbered stands each had been allocated during the ride there. After the first drive, the gentleman would move two places up for each new drive. They waited now, their greatcoats loosely over their shoulders, resting on their shooting sticks until the beaters should start their move along the line, forcing the birds towards them.

In a few moments, a brief whistle sounded and the capped heads of the beaters could be seen working the line, driving up the startled birds. They flew up in a great flurry of beating wings, some straight up, and a few backwards, but most at an angle towards where the hunters were waiting. Then men followed their flight and fired, then, in a single fluid movement immediately handed off the gun to be re-loaded and took a second, loaded one. The retrievers, their noses and ears down and their tails up, took off at once and returned, their mouths full, and what looked like a grin on their faces at all the fun.

After three drives, the long lunch whistle sounded. The piles of dead birds were transported back to the house for hanging. The company would not enjoy them for two days. The men climbed into the gigs once more and were transported to a folly on the highest part of the estate that gave Highmount its name. A previous Lord March had built it specifically for shooting lunches, though a more inconvenient place for the staff to have to transport food and keep it warm could hardly be imagined.

Long trestle tables had been set up, covered with starched linen, silverware and crystal.

The ladies were already there. Cecilia was amongst them, enjoying the wonderful view from the top of the mount and wondering at the effort that had gone into providing all this finery. She had already drunk an unaccustomed lunchtime glass of champagne and was hoping that the meal would be served quite soon, as she had eaten very little breakfast.

She noticed that many of the younger ladies, wearing very modish ensembles, had discarded their cloaks, the better to display their gowns and themselves. She realized that when her aunt had talked about the need for wool in the country, she was only half right. These ladies' gowns may have been of wool but it was of the finest and sheerest, and certainly not chosen for warmth. Some seemed decidedly scanty, and Cecilia wondered that they were not freezing.

She still wore her cloak, though less, it is true, from a need to keep warm than from a feeling of being decidedly underdressed in her made-over skirt and top. Looking around, she realized that wearing a cloak put her in company with the matrons, rather than the women of her own age, but she just shrugged and turned her eyes back to the magnificent view.

She was quite pleased to sit next to her uncle at lunch, for he treated her with kind indifference, and she did not feel it incumbent upon her to make a great deal of conversation with him. On her other side was one of the grandsons of the March family, on his first grown-up shoot and feeling somewhat overawed. She talked to him in a vaguely aunt-like fashion that soon put him at ease, until he was telling her how many birds he had shot, and how many more he had missed. Then he moved on to the prowess of the other gentlemen.

"Tommy Allenby, Lord Broome, you know, is a capital shot. I swear he never misses! But he's so funny about it! He seems to take more time straightening his coat than aiming for the birds, but when he does fire, lord! they just tumble out of the sky! I wish I knew his secret!"

"Which one is Lord Broome?" asked Cecilia, intrigued, and was astonished when her neighbor pointed to the person she recognized as the dandy from the day before.

"You mean the gentleman in grey?"

He was easy to pick out, since most of the other sportsmen wore shapeless or bunched up coats in mixtures of brown and black. Compared with them, he looked as if he had just stepped out of his dressing room. When assured that it was indeed he, she looked back at him, just in time for him to turn to her end of the table and catch her eye. She blushed at being caught so obviously staring, but he gave her a most charming smile and a slight nod of the head. Her heart gave a ridiculous leap and she looked down at her plate in confusion.

When she had the courage to peep back at him, he was talking to his neighbor, one of the matrons who was also still wearing her cloak. Annoyed with herself for reacting as she had, she chastised herself.

"He probably put me in the same category as his neighbor," she thought. "An old fuddy-duddy who he can smile at without her making anything of it".

Deliberately going nowhere near the group of gentlemen the Earl always seemed to be in the midst of, and still wanting to avoid her would-be suitor, Cecilia joined the first group of ladies going back to Highmount House. Most of them went to lie down or perhaps to gossip in their rooms, but she decided it was too nice a day to stay inside and went for a long walk until tea. But the memory of the smile stayed with her all afternoon.

Chapter Five

Tommy kept to his plan of being late downstairs for the pre-dinner gathering. He would willingly forgo a sherry for the benefit of avoiding Pamela Smith, her doe eyes and her shrill voice.

He did not linger over his bath; he took his customary forty-five minutes, which did, it must be said lest this seems excessive, include the filing of his nails. The gentle pulling on of his linen shirt with the highly starched collars and blue satin britches was, however, an affair not to be hurried, nor yet were the donning of his blue and silver striped waistcoat, the slipping on of his glossy evening shoes or the nice arrangement of his golden waves into a state of careful disorder. But where time could never be spared was in the fixing of his neckcloth. His valet held his breath as his master carefully folded the foot-wide muslin and draped it around his neck with just the right mixture of speed and care that would achieve a perfect fall of folds. Once creased, the neckcloth could never be re-used. It would be thrown to the floor and the process begun again afresh. This evening, the gods smiled upon them and it took only three attempts. The wonderful arrangement was fixed with a sapphire-headed pin and his lordship helped into his coat, a marvelous silver confection with a lining of the same blue as his britches, that fit his form as if molded there by an artist.

It wanted but ten minutes of seven, the hour, since they kept early hours in the country, at which dinner was invariably served at Highmount, when the Lord Thomas Allenby finally presented himself to an amazed and flattering crowd.

Cecilia also came down late and for much the same reason. She knew Miles Rowntree would be looking for her again. Fortunately, when she had asked her aunt, that lady had assured her that people were never seated next to each other more than once at a weekend party, so she was safe from him during dinner. She slipped into the drawing room when she judged it late enough, but was nonetheless already there when Tommy arrived in a blaze of blue and silver.

She was wearing one of her rather drab silk evening gowns, in the grey she almost always chose, and had put the bronze shawl around her shoulders again. She wore her mother's pearl earrings, not because she thought they especially suited her, or because they looked well with the rest of her outfit, but because they were the only pair she owned. In fact, they looked very nice.

She had piled her abundant hair on top of her head and pinned it as best she could, but a few escaping ringlets fell in front of her ears and the pearls formed a nice contrast to their dark glossiness. The color of the shawl drew out the golden-brown highlights in her hair and gave a glow to her complexion. A couple of the other young ladies, dressed far more fashionably than she and who had dismissed her on sight the previous day as being no competition for their prettiness — besides, she was so tall! — were quite struck by her appearance this evening. She was certainly not beautiful, and her gown, what they could see of it, was deplorable, but with her hair, which, despite the prevailing fashion, she had never had cropped at the sides, her long neck and her stately physique, she was hard to ignore. There was, as her uncle had said, something about her.

However, not knowing her appearance had met with something like muted approval, Cecilia felt as much out of place as she had the day before, and wished she could escape the same way. The pleasant anticipation she had experienced before coming to Highmount had given way to the same sense she always had, of not belonging, of being different, of being always on the outside looking in. She hid behind the same potted palm and watched her fellows hailing each other in friendship.

Lady March had buttonholed Tommy as he arrived and berated him in the piercing voice peculiar to women of rank of a certain age.

"Good God, Tommy!" she said as she beheld him in all his splendor. "You must think you are at Versailles twenty years ago. They sent men to the guillotine for less!"

Tommy smiled and bent over her hand. "But think, my dear lady, how the maidens would have cried to see such perfection wheeled thither in a tumbril! It might have been almost worth it, to create for posterity such a picture; a man in a silver coat, with shining white smallclothes, led through a crowd of ill-dressed, ragged ruffians who, in their hearts, knew he was, and would forever be, their superior. It would have been worthy of a Delacroix, were he not such a damned Republican."

"I don't know what you're talking about, you silly boy! Get yourself a sherry, if you want one. We'll be going in in a minute."

"I'll wait for the burgundy. Please tell me I am to have the honor of taking you in this evening? My heart was broken yesterday when I had to cede place to old Devonshire. His waistcoat looked as if it had been used to line the bottom of a birdcage!"

"Don't be absurd! Lord Devonshire is your elder and better. And tonight you will take in Miss Beaumaris. Your grandmother desired it of me."

"Elder, yes; better, no. I refuse to accept as a better a man who dresses like that. And who is Miss Beaumaris? I feel sure I've heard the name, but cannot put a face to it."

"But you are too ridiculous! That is the young lady your grandmother sent you here to meet. You said so yourself only yesterday, after hiding in the billiard room all night."

"Oh yes," replied Tommy, in a tone of resignation. "I suppose I'll have to meet her sooner or later, so it may as well be sooner."

His hostess led him across the room to where Cecilia was attempting to hide. Behind the palm, it was only because of her height that she was visible at all. She was astonished when Lady March brought to her the man whose smile had unwillingly occupied her thoughts all afternoon. As their hostess made the introductions, he bowed and smiled at her again. He gave no indication that he had seen her before. Then the butler came into the room and caught his mistress's eye.

"Tommy will take you into dinner, my dear," she said to Cecilia, before leaving them together.

"Oh, I'm sure ... that is, do not feel obliged ...," she began.

"You don't understand, Miss Beaumaris," answered the Earl, taking her hand and placing it on his arm. "Neither of us has any choice in the matter. Lady March has ordained it. Besides," he added quickly, conscious that his words may have sounded a little rude, "I am delighted to make your acquaintance. I saw you at lunch did I not?" He began leading her towards the door, holding back a little, to let the crush subside.

So he *did* recognize her! Cecilia did not know whether to be embarrassed or gratified. She decided to be plain.

"Yes, the person next to me had pointed you out as being the best shot, and I was just looking to see whom he meant. It must have looked as if I was staring, excuse me." She looked him straight in the eye.

Tommy was suddenly conscious of two things: the low, musical pitch of her voice, and the fact that she was almost as tall as he. Although not an exceptionally tall man, at just over six feet, he was accustomed to looking down at the girls he met, and accustomed, too, to their peeping up at him through their lashes. It was a trick they must all learn at their mother's knee, he had decided. This was the first time in his life a woman had looked at him just as another man would, with no coquetry, no guile, just a straightforward gaze. He found it a little unnerving.

"Er, no… no need to apologize. It could happen to anyone." Then, recovering his sangfroid, "I just thought how well the feather in your bonnet matched your dark eyes." He looked straight into them. "Now I see they are really quite out of the common way, dark brown but flecked with gold. But perhaps it is your shawl that makes them appear so."

Although she was certain she was just the latest beneficiary of an accomplished flirt, Cecilia decided there and then to wear that shawl every day of her life. She was saved from having to answer by the butler leading Tommy to their places at table. They were to be seated side by side. She did not know whether to be glad or sorry.

For the first half of the dinner, Cecilia was obliged, as was customary, to talk to the person on her right. He turned out to be the chaplain of the Highmount estate, an elderly, gentle man who looked as if he was hungry, which, indeed, he was. His wife, who sat opposite, was a thin, rather grey woman who made a point, it seemed to Cecilia, of eating nearly nothing. It turned out that she was opposed to the consumption of flesh and therefore had a diet of mostly vegetables, which she inflicted on her husband. The chaplain told her this, in his gentle way, without, however, appearing to place any blame upon his wife.

"I'm sure she is right," he explained. "Vegetables are much easier to produce and much kinder to prepare than animals. It's just that one does, from time to time, so desire a good piece of meat!"

Since the fish pie had at that point been removed and the footmen were handing down platters of what looked like thick pieces of roast beef, the chaplain suited his action to his words, and took a large helping. This was followed by a number of side dishes, including leeks with bread sauce, nests of potato filled with browned onions and livers in pastry cases, which she was entertained to see him consume in large quantities, out of all proportion to his spare frame.

The talk of food naturally led to a discussion of those who had much less, and thence to the question of the poor and ultimately, the education of poor girls. Cecilia had tried to settle her nerves by drinking a glass of whatever the wine was that was put before her and was now feeling less reserved than she customarily felt at a dinner party. The chaplain was so gently attentive that she found herself telling him enthusiastically all about her plan to open a school in London's East End.

He was most struck by her plan and said he wished more persons of means would think as she did. He spoke of the evils that preyed on young women especially when they left their villages to find work in the cities. Whereas at home they might find charity in the local parish, in the city everyone was a stranger. His views were so close to her own that she was disappointed when, after the first course, she had to turn her attention to the Earl on the other side.

The combination of talking to the chaplain and the unaccustomed glass of wine had made Cecilia forget her earlier embarrassment with Lord Tommy. She could face her left-hand neighbor with objectivity. How silly, she said to herself, as the first course was cleared, to be so smitten by a smile! And a smile from a dandy who probably spent more on a coat he might only wear once, than a poor family had to feed their children for a year.

So when she turned to him, instead of finding his good looks and engaging address appealing, she found him almost despicable. It was true that his manners were excellent. He tried to find innocuous subjects on which they might converse unexceptionally: the continuing good weather, the beauty of the countryside, the excellence of the meal. But convinced of his worthlessness, she answered only mechanically.

Tommy had been aware of her chatting freely in her well-modulated voice to the gentleman on her right, and was surprised when she turned at last to him, that she appeared not to want to talk to him. She answered his questions with little more than yes or no, and volunteered nearly nothing in return. He was a man of considerable address and found her unwillingness to participate in his lighthearted conversation puzzling. Her calm gaze before dinner had piqued his interest.

He had never met anyone like this unusual young woman with her glorious head of hair, dark eyes and tall, stately carriage.

Her shawl had slipped from her shoulders and in the covert looks he had stolen at her while she was talking on the other side, he saw that her gown was lamentable, both in color and shape. He was well known amongst the young women of the *ton* for his impeccable taste in the matter of female attire. Now he found himself wishing he had the dressing of her. But if he had to describe her attitude towards him, he would have said that it bordered on dislike. In what way, he wondered, had he offended her? Finally, he decided to be blunt.

"What have I done, Miss Beaumaris, that you should so dislike talking to me?" he said calmly.

"I don't … that is, you haven't … I can't imagine what you mean, Lord Broome," she said, taken entirely by surprise.

"I think you do," he replied, gently. "I heard you carrying on an enthusiastic conversation with your other partner, but to me you have uttered only monosyllables or the merest platitudes. If I have offended you in some way, I beg you to tell me, so that I may put it right."

Luckily for Cecilia, before she could respond, the footman offered her a platter of what looked like mutton with capers. Since she had eaten as much mutton as she hoped ever to see since living with her aunt and uncle, she took a very small helping, and then only toyed with it on her plate.

"Quite right, Miss Beaumaris," said Tommy with a smile after the footman had moved on. "Mutton is one of those dishes one should avoid wherever possible. Now, where were we? Oh yes, you were going to tell me why you don't like me."

This was said in such a friendly way that Cecilia was put off balance. But the footman was back, this time with a sliced pork pie surrounded by stewed apples. She helped herself mechanically, furiously thinking how she was going to answer his lordship's question. When she looked down at her plate, she saw she had taken a whole slice of pie and a quantity of apples.

"Oh dear!" she exclaimed, "I can't possibly eat all this!"

"Then don't." said his lordship, reasonably.

"But that seems wicked, when there are people without enough to eat," protested Cecilia.

"Ah!" responded Tommy, putting a small slice of pie into his mouth. He chewed and swallowed. "But eating more than you wish to, or eating something you do not care for, will not put food into the mouths of those unfortunate people. All we end up with is everyone being unhappy: you for being over-full and the starving for still being hungry." He took a sip from his wine glass.

"That is precisely the sort of argument I would expect someone like you to make," retorted Cecilia before she could stop herself.

"Someone like me?" replied Tommy, with a lift of his eyebrow. "But are you not someone like me? You are here at the same invitation as I, conversing with the same people as I, enjoying the same entertainment as I, eating the same meal as I."

Cecilia spoke angrily before she had time to think. "I could not be less like you, my lord! She returned to her earlier thought, "I do not wear upon my back a coat that probably cost more than a working family in London may earn in a twelvemonth!"

"Ah, I am beginning to perceive why you dislike me." commented his lordship, in no way disturbed by her rudeness. "You think I am one of those frippery fellows who thinks of nothing but his raiment. One who would no doubt step over a starving child to reach the door of his tailor's establishment. Hmm..." he appeared to contemplate the question for a moment. "Would I, I wonder, step over a starving child in such circumstances? Perhaps if I were anxious to take possession of a very special coat, like this one, for instance. Don't you think it would be worth it?" His eyes danced.

In spite of the fact that he was clearly only teasing her, the question made her even angrier. "Don't be ridiculous!" she snapped. "You know you are talking nonsense!"

"But I was taught that the dinner table with strangers was not the place to enter into personal discussions, and certainly not to cast animadversions upon one's neighbor's sartorial choices."

Of course, Cecilia had been taught exactly the same and she by now very much regretted her outburst. She was desperate to extricate herself from the abominable situation her sharp tongue, combined with the glasses of wine, had put her in.

"I understand that you wish to put me in my place for my unwarranted outburst," she said rapidly. "All I can do is apologize for saying what I did. It is in no way any business of mine how you choose to dress. Now please can we end this dreadful dialog."

"Miss Beaumaris! Absolve me, I beg you, of any attempt to *put you in your place*, as you term it! replied her tormentor, who had, in fact, conceived a most unusual desire to do precisely that to this critical young woman. "I have merely been trying to understand your dislike of me, and I think I may say, I have now done so. You consider me a person with more money than sense, unashamedly selfish and with no social conscience. Am I not right?"

This was said with another of the Earl's charming smiles, and it was that, together with the knowledge that he had pinpointed with absolute accuracy her opinion of him, that finally undid Cecilia.

"Please, my lord," she said in a low voice, trying to keep her voice even, though she felt a restriction at the back of her throat, "please do not continue in this vein. I have apologized and I apologize again. I should not have said what I did. I beg you to let me eat the rest of my meal quietly as I…I do not wish to make a spectacle of myself," she finished in a low voice, looking at him beseechingly, her eyes bright with unshed tears.

Tommy saw them and was ashamed. He knew what he had done. He gave a brief nod of agreement, and turned his attention to his dinner. After a minute, he stole a look at her profile and was admiring her long neck and lustrous hair, set off by the pearls, when he was dismayed to see a single tear drop onto her plate. He was not by nature unkind and the thought that he had brought this strange young woman to tears affected him powerfully.

"Do not allow it to upset you," he said very quietly, without turning his head, "It is really of no consequence, you know."

But she gave no sign she had heard him.

Chapter Six

Unutterably relieved when the ladies left the gentlemen to their port, Cecilia went immediately up to her room, where her emotions finally got the better of her. She wept as she could not remember weeping in her life before. She was obliged to bring her bed pillow to her face to suffocate her sobbing, and it was some minutes before she could gain control of herself. At length her passion wore itself out, and, having washed her face and taken a drink of cool water from the jug on the washstand, she sat on the edge of her bed for some time until her breathing returned to normal. It was fully dark by now, and, as she could hear the maids coming in to light the candles, she slipped out of her room and down the stairs. She knew she could not disappear for the second night in a row. Her aunt had already rebuked her that morning.

"Really, Cecilia! When one is invited to the country for the weekend, one is obliged to do one's part by joining in! It simply is not done to disappear! Miles Rowntree was looking for you. One may guess why." She had looked arch. "Even if you mean to refuse his offer, though I don't know why you should, as he seems most eligible, you must be polite enough to meet him. Do not, I pray you, wander off again!"

The gentlemen had already arrived by the time she entered the drawing room, and she saw Miles Rowntree notice her immediately. He came over.

"Miss Beaumaris," he said with a bow. "I have been trying to obtain a few minutes with you since last evening. 'Pon my word! One would almost think you were avoiding me!"

"Mr. Rowntree," she said in a low voice. "I pray you, not here. Won't you walk outside with me for a moment? See, the French doors have been opened and others are enjoying the lovely night."

"For a moment or two, then, if you insist," he said, "though I do not find the night air salubrious." He gave a weak cough. "My mother is forever warning me not to venture outside after the sun has gone down. My chest, the damp, you know."

But as Cecilia was already moving forward, he had no choice but to follow her out onto the terrace, where a few of the gentlemen were smoking cigars and their ladies were clustered together, chatting. She led him down the steps in the direction she had gone the night before, and when they were sufficiently out of sight, reluctantly turned to him.

"Miss Beaumaris," he began. "You cannot be ignorant of the feelings I have for you. I believe I have treated you with singularity on the occasions of our meeting in recent weeks."

He appeared to be expecting some sort of confirmation, so Cecilia responded, "Yes, but I must tell you, Mr. Rowntree …"

But she got no further. He took both her hands and declared, "Give me leave to express the affection and respect I feel for you. You are not in your first youth, I know, and you do not aspire to the modishness one sees in other young women. Indeed, you have not been used to a society such as you now enjoy. But in spite of this, I am persuaded you are the partner I would choose above all others. I therefore ask you to do me the honor of becoming my wife."

Cecilia, already exasperated with having to deal with yet another unwanted proposal, was stung to anger by this enumeration of her shortcomings. After her dinner table experience, her temper was less strictly guarded than it might otherwise have been.

"When you were listing the drawbacks associated with my person," she answered tartly, "I wonder whether, if you had added my lack of fortune, you would have seen fit to approach me at all!"

Her suitor was taken aback, "Your lack of fortune? But I thought …"

"You thought I had money," she interrupted scornfully. "And consideration of it outweighed all the shortcomings you have just enumerated. This is a rumor that has been circulating ever since I came on the town, in spite of my attempts to scotch it. But I assure you, I am not possessed of a fortune. I have a mere competence left by my parents. No more. I'm therefore sure, Mr. Rowntree, that when you add that to the manifold other inconveniences associated with me, you would like to withdraw your offer. But I shall save you the embarrassment. No, Mr. Rowntree, with or without a fortune, I will not marry you. I recommend you find a woman younger, more modish and more accustomed to … *society*," this said with awful emphasis, "than I. Now I wish you good night."

She began to stride off around the side of the house, but stopped and turned back. "And, furthermore, may I also recommend that when you find a woman to whom you wish to offer the protection of your name, you talk to her not of *affection* and *respect*, but of love. No woman wishes to think she fills her would-be husband's breast with those feeble emotions!"

Cecilia turned again and walked on swiftly, her bosom heaving with indignation. She saw that she was passing the library once more, and, again, it was empty, with the dull glow of the fire and a single half-lit chandelier providing a muted light. Making up her mind, she entered the house by the same door as the evening before, walked past what was clearly the billiard room, for although the door was closed, she could hear the clamor of raised masculine voices, to the door of what she thought must be the library. Sure enough, when she opened it, the low light and indefinable smell of old books told her she was right.

She entered and closed the door firmly behind her, but, still too incensed to sit down, began to pace across the room, away from the low glow of the fire, in front of which two high-backed wing chairs were placed.

"No longer young, not modish, not used to society, that's how he sees me!" she said out loud to herself. "The affection and respect I feel for you! Good God, what a bore! Marry him! I should think not, indeed! Oh, how many more of these stupid proposals do I have to endure? If there were a sharp paper knife here somewhere, I swear I should put an end to my existence!"

She walked towards the chairs in front of the fire, as if in search of one.

"Pray do not do anything rash!" came a voice well known to her, and rising from behind the wings of one of the chairs in front of the fire were the countenance and then the form of Thomas Allenby, Earl of Broome.

"If you must do something of the sort, dear Miss Beaumaris, have a thought to those of us who would be required to bring you aid. Imagine the state of my coat if I were obliged to raise your bloody head from the carpet! And should I be obliged to cradle your head on my bosom, consider, I implore you, the detriment to my waistcoat! Though you may consider it just retribution for my appalling behavior at dinner, I beg you not to do it!"

Knowing he had caused Miss Beaumaris to shed a tear had weighed heavily on Tommy's conscience, and he had sought her out as soon as he could after the gentlemen rejoined the ladies. He had not seen her at first, and then when he did, she was leading Miles Rowntree out onto the terrace. The sight gave him a pang. What attracted her in that prosy bore, he wondered. Surely she could see through his sense of self-importance to the cosseted mama's boy that lay beneath.

He had then taken himself off to the billiard room, which, in spite of Lady March's threat had not been locked, but found his spirits too oppressed to enjoy the rowdy bonhomie there. Finally, he had poured himself a generous glass of his host's brandy and sought the quiet of the library. He knew the company at Highmount was not bookish and it would probably be empty.

He settled himself in front of the low fire and began to examine his conscience, in a way the chaplain at Thyford had frequently advised when he was a boy, but which he had rarely attempted. Why had he deliberately set out to discountenance Miss Beaumaris? It was most unlike him. Was it because she had said what others would like to say but dare not? His position in the *ton* was unassailable. He was wealthy, good looking, popular, had the entrée everywhere and was consequently courted rather than criticized. This he knew. Now he wondered whether it had engendered in him the conceit that was, as he remembered from his school days where, in spite of his outward frivolity, he had gleaned an idea or two, the downfall of men much greater than he.

He was mulling over these imponderables when the door had opened and the object of his musings had walked in, talking to herself in obvious agitation. She obviously thought the room was empty. He had wanted to make himself known, but did not like to interrupt her. Perhaps she would go away again, none the wiser. But then she had come towards where he was sitting and he had been forced to disclose himself.

To do her credit, Miss Beaumaris did not shriek with alarm or run away. "My lord!" she said in her low voice, though with obvious displeasure. "It wanted but this to make my evening complete! Is it your habit to listen to private thoughts uttered by persons who think they are alone?"

"Not at all, Miss Beaumaris. I was trying to think how to make myself known to you when you started talking about putting a period to your existence with a sharp paper knife. I confess I was shocked into speech before thinking."

"And how ironic that your first thoughts should have been about your coat. It really seems to occupy your thoughts more than anyone could consider reasonable. It has been the cause of all this evening's troubles. Really, your coat is beginning to take on mythic proportions!"

Suddenly the ridiculousness of the situation struck her, and before she knew what she was doing, she started to laugh. It was doubtless a reaction to the emotional upheavals of the previous couple of hours, but she found she could not stop. She laughed and laughed, collapsing into one of the chairs and finally reaching for a handkerchief in her reticule to wipe away the tears that were by now coursing down her cheeks. But rummage as she might in the depths, she could not find one.

"Allow me," said her companion cheerfully, and handed her a large, snow white piece of linen with an ornate B embroidered in the corner.

"Ar...are you s...sure?" choked Cecilia, trying to control both herself, "Are you sure you don't want to protect it as much as ... as ... your c...c...coat?" and she went off into another peal of laughter.

It is impossible to look at someone laughing without laughing oneself, and it was not long before Tommy was as helpless with mirth as she. They only had to look at one another to start up again. They sat in their chairs, both laughing helplessly. When the paroxysms at last seemed to be diminishing, Tommy spoke first, attempting a seriousness of tone that was almost impossible, as his companion kept hiccupping and had to practically stuff the handkerchief in her mouth to stop bursting out again.

"Miss Beaumaris. I cannot tell you how glad I am to see you enjoying such a good joke when I have been sitting here wondering how to make amends for my atrocious behavior earlier. I am truly sorry for having upset you, and I cannot explain why I did it, except to say that I suppose I disliked being made to see myself for the frippery fellow I am."

Cecilia was at last sobered. "My lord," she replied, swallowing convulsively and folding and refolding the mangled handkerchief in her lap, "please do not apologize. It is I who was at fault. I was inexcusably rude. If I made you out to be a frippery fellow, I also made myself out to be the most stiff-necked, accusatory and disagreeable female on the face of the earth. Let us agree that we are neither of these things and forget all about it."

"Willingly," said Tommy, "My hand on it." He held out his hand, and when she took it, held hers for a moment, looking at her. Her eyes were red and her hair was coming loose from its pins. She looked vulnerable and much younger. "Now we are old friends," he said at last, releasing her hand, "you will not mind my asking what had you so overwrought when you came into the library just now."

"Oh, it was just another offer of marriage, even less attractive than the last. You see," she said, the sense of closeness engendered by laughing oneself to tears with someone else overcoming her reluctance to confide in anyone, "everyone thinks I have a fortune. I think my uncle may have started the rumor. They want to be rid of me and since a too-tall, too-old, too-outspoken female with no pretensions to beauty and no money is unlikely to receive any offers, they invented the fortune to attract some. You would be amazed how many men have offered me marriage because of it. But you know, not one of them has mentioned the word *love*. I have been assured of affection and respect. Bah! Who wants that? But it doesn't matter, as I have no intention of marrying anyone. In a few months, when I am twenty-five, I shall have the disposition of the competence my parents left me. At that time, I plan to have my own establishment and form some sort of school for the education of poor girls in the City. I just wish I could stop these would-be suitors. Nothing I say seems to deter them. They think I am being coy, or hoping to make myself all the more desirable by refusing them. It's driving me mad! The latest assault came this evening from Miles Rowntree. It was awful. It made me so cross and coming on top of our ... our disagreement at dinner, I was overwrought. I'm sorry you had to witness it."

Tommy looked at her. "First let me say, your description of yourself in no way accords with the person I see sitting opposite me. You are neither too tall nor too old. Your figure is perfect for your height and your carriage gives you a rare dignity. It is true you are outspoken, but that is tempered by generosity, as we see from what you have said about your plans, and we both know you have a sense of humor. As for your beauty, I, Tommy Allenby, well-known connoisseur of the female sex, tell you that you have a beauty that is not of the common sort. You will be lovely when you are ninety and you would be lovely now if someone with taste were to guide you in the purchase of your gowns. Good God, woman, with your inches, your hair and your eyes you could put them all to shame! But not wearing that dreadful dull grey. If you must wear grey, let it be with a blue undertone. Better still, wear lilac or moss green. Yellow-gold would do as well," he added as an afterthought, looking at her appraisingly.

Cecilia looked at him in amazement. No one had ever suggested she was lovely. No one had ever said her inches were an advantage, and as for her eyes and hair, she had always secretly longed to be blond and blue-eyed, like her classmates at Mrs. Farridge's establishment who, within months of leaving, always came back wearing engagement rings. Her friend Laura Warren had always said she could make more of herself, and she had heard herself described as quite good-looking, a lukewarm term she put in the same category as affection and respect. She was at a loss to answer him.

"Th...thank you," she said finally. "I...I rarely buy new clothes but if I do, I shall bear in mind what you say."

"Do," he replied. "I try to get m'sisters never buy anything without consulting me. They're both blond like me and used to persist in wearing puce, until I simply had to cut them dead when they wore it. Why is it that blonds always think that some sort of violent pink is just the thing? Pale pink, at the limit. Preferably, no pink at all! Did you see Pamela Smith, for instance?"

"Was she the girl hanging on your arm yesterday?"

"Yes. Yaller hair and rose-pink! She always wears it. Put it together with a voice that would shatter glass and you have the stuff of nightmares!"

"It looked as if you were being very nice to her."

"Oh well, you know, doesn't do to be rude. Except, of course," he added with a twinkle, "to too-tall, too-old, too-outspoken girls of no fortune or pretensions to beauty who happen to sit next to you at dinner."

Cecilia laughed. "And threaten to kill themselves with a paper knife and leave you to deal with the corpse in your new coat!"

Tommy laughed too. "Precisely! We understand each other perfectly. But then, of course, we are old friends."

He was quiet for a moment. Then he said, "Look here, Miss Beaumaris, I think we can do each other some good. My grandmother is after me to get married. Provide an heir, that sort of thing. I'm the only male, got two sisters. Never leaves me alone. You have these dratted fellers trying to marry you for money you don't have. Never leave you alone. Why don't we announce our betrothal? Shut 'em all up. A few months of peace until you get your inheritance, then ... well, you can decide we don't suit and call it off. What do you say?"

Cecilia was still smiling about their last exchange and did not think she had heard aright. *"What* did you say? I thought you suggested we become betrothed, but I must have misheard."

"No, you did not mishear. I did suggest it. That way people will leave us alone. It seems an excellent plan to me. We understand each other, and have shaken hands on our friendship. Not many betrothals are based on such a foundation, I'll wager."

"But, but ..." stuttered Cecilia. "No one would believe it! You are, well, you are a well-known figure in the *ton* and I, I'm a nobody, a less than nobody! People would laugh!"

"Come now, Miss Beaumaris, don't tell me you are afraid of people laughing? I don't believe you give a fig what people think. Well, neither do I. Besides, I've been laughed at for years. It has served me in very good stead. No one expects anything of me as a result. They just say 'Oh, it's only old Tommy, take no notice!'"

Cecilia was dumbfounded. He must be joking! But one look at his face convinced her he was serious. And then she laughed again.

"Well, it would certainly make my aunt and uncle happy, but I can't believe your grandmother would be *aux anges* to see you connected to me."

"But it was she who sent me here specifically to meet you! Her exact words were, *don't come back without a betrothal in your pocket.* Well, for once I shall not disappoint her. Do say you will, Miss Beaumaris! Shall I address you on bended knee?"

"No, no, of course not! It would not be a real engagement in any case. But very well, Lord Broome, I accept! Let us be betrothed." She shrugged, "Why not, after all? It can't be any worse than constant proposals."

Tommy stood up and made her a graceful bow. "I should now say you make me the happiest of men, Miss Beaumaris, and indeed, you do, though not for the usual reasons. By the way, what is your name? It would be useful to know, under the circumstances."

Cecilia could not help but laugh. She held out her hand. "Cecilia. My Christian name is Cecilia. Please don't call me Cecily as many people do, even one gentleman who proposed to me."

Tommy took her hand and brought her fingers to his lips. "Cecilia. A lovely name for a lovely woman. I most certainly shall not call you anything else. You call me Tommy. Everyone does, except my grandmother when she's vexed with me. If you want the whole mouthful, it's Thomas Algernon Wymering Allenby, fourth Earl of Broome. I try to forget it as much as I can. Do you have any other names I should know? For the notice in the newspapers, you know."

"The newspapers?" repeated Cecilia, startled. "Oh, yes, I suppose we shall have to put something in. My full name is Cecilia Anne Beaumaris. Anne was my mother's name. My father was the Honorable Edmund Beaumaris." She was quiet for a moment, then said, as a thought struck her, "But please, don't say anything while we are here. I don't think I could stand the outcry."

"Very well. Come, let's go into the drawing room now. Your eyes are a little red from the tears of joy you have shed at my proposal and your slightly disheveled coiffure looks as though I may have caught you in a fierce embrace. All to the good.

People will remember it after they read the announcement and say 'Aha! That's what they were up to!'"

A blush suffused Cecilia's face in spite of herself, so that the picture they presented as they came together into the drawing room was exactly what Tommy had described.

Chapter Seven

With complete assurance, Tommy led Cecilia to a sofa, where he sat next to her for the next half hour, telling her scurrilous stories about all the other people in the room, their relationships with each other, legitimate or clandestine; whom she might expect to meet creeping between bedrooms if she chose to venture onto the upstairs landing at about two in the morning; the maids' discovery on bringing in morning tea some years ago, of one of the now formidable matrons asleep in bed with a man who most certainly was not her husband, who when he awoke, took one look at her and said, "My God! I thought it couldn't be Louisa (his wife). She never had such energy!" Her closeted upbringing told her she should be scandalized, but Tommy was such an amusing raconteur that she found herself laughing out loud.

Lady March suddenly clapped her hands and called to Tommy in her piercing voice, "Tommy, come and play a tune or two on the piano. Some of the younger set want to dance."

Cecilia heard him mutter "Dammit!" and asked in surprise, "Do you play?"

"Oh, just a few bits and pieces, you know. Unfortunately, our hostess knows it. She and my grandmother are thick as thieves. Gran probably told her to make me play to keep me out of the billiard room."

But he rose with every appearance of willingness and wandered over to the piano, while the footmen, directed by their mistress, removed chairs and the rug from that end of the room. He seated himself carefully and smoothed out the skirts of his coat, picking off a minute piece of fluff. Then he ran his fingers over the keys and began to play the Belle Assemblée March that traditionally presented all the dancers at the start.

No one approached her to dance, a circumstance to which she had become accustomed since her introduction into London society. The gentlemen who had subsequently asked for her hand would usually ask her to dance if the occasion arose, but since she had refused them all, they avoided her. Other gentlemen were no doubt put off by her height and her cool demeanor.

But she sat happily enough watching Tommy play. His fingers seemed to glide effortlessly over the keys, and she thought his description of his skills had been self-deprecating, to say the least. After the March, he played the Boulanger, a simple dance that Cecilia had learned at school. Miss Farridge rightly considered the ability to dance a prerequisite for the graduates of her Academy, and it had always been one of Cecilia's favorite parts of the curriculum. That was followed by the Cotillion, an old-fashioned dance that had largely been replaced by the Quadrille in the smart ballrooms in town. But whereas the latter had a variety of figures which could be introduced at will and needed to be worked out in advance by a dance master, the Cotillion used repeating figures that most people knew. Next came two Reels – energetic skipping affairs, the second of which Tommy played faster and faster until there was almost total chaos.

"I need a break," he announced when the second came to its riotous conclusion. Amid laughter and demands for more, and came back through the throng to Cecilia.

"I hope your sitting here all alone doesn't mean you don't like to dance," he said.

"No, I like it very much but I find my extra inches are a deterrent to many men."

"Not to me," he replied. "Do you waltz?"

She nodded. "Yes, I do, or at least I know the steps ... but backwards. You see," she explained ruefully, "I was by far the tallest girl at school, so I mostly had to be the man."

"Well, you're not taller than me! I hope you're not suggesting I be the woman!" laughed Tommy.

"Of course not!" Cecilia joined in his laughter. "But you may find I try to push you instead of your pushing me!"

"I do not push, I gently guide," replied Tommy with a lift of his eyebrows, "and I shall not allow you to push me. In fact, I hope you will put only the lightest of touches on my coat. I'm worried about its surface being chafed."

"But of course," said Cecilia with a straight face. "It would be sacrilege to mar its mythical perfection."

One of the young bucks Cecilia recognized from the billiard room hailed his lordship from across the room and started to cross over.

"Hey, Tommy! How many you bag today? I heard you'd got over fifty!"

"I've no idea, Bunty. Didn't count. How about you? Good shooting?"

"Oh, so-so, you know. My aim seemed off."

He approached them and bowed to Cecilia "Miss Beaumaris, your most obedient." Then, turning back to Tommy, "All that brandy the night before, I expect. Didn't seem to bother you, though."

"I put it down to clean living and a study of the scriptures. In the library, examining m' conscience and that sort of thing. Ask Miss Beaumaris, she'll tell you."

"Oh, is that what you were doing in there? Never heard it called that before! Well, tol-lol, I'm off to dance with Pam. I heard something about a waltz."

He bowed to Cecilia who had blushed at the reference to the library. Tommy grinned and squeezed her hand.

By that time, the old governess of the house had been unearthed and she declared herself ready to play, so long as it was not too fast. The young people were only too eager to inform her that a slow waltz was exactly what was required. Tommy led his betrothed onto the floor and put his hand firmly in the small of her back. In deference to his coat, she lay her right hand on his upper arm with the lightest of pressure. They began a very slow waltz and Cecilia found that what his lordship had said was right. He did not push, in fact he seemed to exert no pressure at all, but nonetheless her feet were guided in the right way, and she soon became accustomed to going backwards to where at school she had gone forward.

She had never been so close to a man before. His masculine scent, a combination of lime, bay and something indefinable, met her nostrils and she realized that although he was only three or four inches taller than she, his shoulders were much broader, and his arms much bigger. In spite of her delicate touch on his coat, she could feel his muscles beneath the silk.

For the first time in her life, she felt almost fragile. It was a wonderful feeling, and she felt she could dance forever.

After the waltz came the Sir Roger de Coverley which always signaled the end of the dancing. The betrothed couple danced that together too. Quite soon after that, the tea tray was brought in. The second evening thus passed much more pleasantly than the first, and Cecilia went up to bed in something of a daze. Worn out by the conflicting emotions of the day, she fell into a sound sleep.

She was awoken the following morning by the entrance of her aunt. This lady was generally not of matitudinal habits, and Cecilia was surprised to see her.

"My dear!" she said, "I felt I simply had to come to find out what on earth you were about yesterday evening. One minute you were leaving the room with Miles Rowntree and the next coming back in with Tommy Allenby. If one didn't know you better, such behavior could only be characterized as *fast*!"

Cecilia gave what was, to her ears, an unconvincing laugh. "Oh aunt! It was pure happenstance. It's true I left the room with Mr. Rowntree. He proposed, of course, a thing I had been trying to avoid, and I left him to return to the house by a side door. I ... er met Lord Broome on the way back and he was kind enough to walk with me."

"But he sat and talked to you for a full thirty minutes and then waltzed with you! You cannot deny that was the most particular attention! I pray your head may not be turned! Tommy Allenby! My dear, that is looking very high indeed!"

Cecilia was on the verge of telling her the truth, but she knew that, even if she swore her aunt to secrecy, she would be incapable of keeping it to herself. Word would get out and before that evening everyone would know of it. So she said nothing and after a few minutes, her aunt left her.

She passed the rest of the day alternating between the happiness of being included in the Earl's set, for, while he did not pay her any marked attention, he certainly made sure she was never alone, and the unsettling anticipation of what the revelation of their betrothal might bring. Her simple desire was that, once she was back in London, she would be able to continue her lessons with the maids and plan her new school. She would also ask her parents' man of business to wait on her so that she would finally have a clear idea of what financial means were at her disposal. Most of all, she hoped she would be left alone.

When the party broke up on Monday morning, Tommy sought her out, drew her into a quiet corner and said, "I must tell my grandmother before I do anything else. She would never forgive me if the first she hears of my betrothal is in the newspaper, even though she's been chivvying me any time these last three years. But the announcement will be in the papers by the end of the week. Do not fail me!"

"I fail you?" smiled Cecilia, "don't you think it's more likely the other way round?"

"Not at all! We Allenbys are noted for our stubborn adherence to things. This waistcoat, for instance. I can't tell you how many people have criticized it, but I stick to it. In fact, it's one of my favorites."

Since the garment in question was of purple silk run through with black stripes, Cecilia could only smile. "I think it's a very nice waistcoat, and I'm honored to be compared with it," she said in her musical voice.

"You see, I said we should deal famously together!" he responded, "we do understand each other perfectly. I shall write as soon as I see my way clear. For the moment, goodbye, my dear." He kissed her hand and was gone.

Once they returned to London, Cecilia left it two days before telling her aunt and uncle about her betrothal. Then, at the end of dinner, when the servants had withdrawn, she announced,

"Aunt, uncle, I have something important to tell you. As my aunt knows, over the weekend at Highmount I became acquainted with Tommy Allenby and … and, well, the long and the short of it is that we are betrothed."

Her aunt choked on a sweetmeat she had just conveyed to her mouth and her uncle dropped a silver spoon in which he had been inspecting his teeth for spinach.

Her uncle was the first to recover. "Upon my word, Cecilia! That was quick work! I never took you for … for … well," his voice tailed off and she was never to know what he never took her for.

Her aunt was more succinct. "Rubbish! You must be imagining things my dear!" She went into another fit of choking. When she had recovered, she gasped, "Tommy Allenby has been for years a prime target of girls with a lot more … more, well a lot more to offer than you. Just because he was kind enough to sit and talk and then take a turn on the dance floor with you doesn't mean he proposed!"

"Nevertheless, within a few days you will see a notice of our betrothal in the papers. I wanted to tell you so you might be prepared."

"Well, I hope I may see it, indeed," responded her aunt, her voice heavy with skepticism. "But, I pray you, do not be spreading the word about. I cannot imagine what others will think if they hear such a story."

"I've no intention of spreading the word. In fact, I don't wish to discuss it at all. Now, if you will excuse me, I have letters to attend to."

In fact, Cecilia had received two letters. The first was from Mr. John Pounds, the cobbler in Portsmouth who ran a school for the poor.

Portsmouth

Dear Miss Beaumaris,

I received your letter with great pleasure. There is no greater calling than to educate the young, especially the poor who would otherwise never have a chance.

You know, I believe, that I began my school after suffering an accident in the dockyard when I was fifteen, in which, though I lost the use of my legs, I was lucky to be spared my life. I say lucky to be spared, but I was at first so angry and miserable at the loss of the use of my limbs that I was tempted to complete the job that the accident had not. It was many months before I could lift my head from my sorrows and look around me. When I did, I saw how I could give thanks for the good fortune that had saved me.

I could not and cannot walk without assistance, but I still had the use of my hands, and of my brain. I had myself received an education, my good father (himself a shipwright in the dockyard) being able to pay the small fee that was then (and still is) demanded by the Portsmouth Beneficial Society School. There I learned to read and write (handwriting was indeed, one of the principal subjects) and do such arithmetic as a working man might need. I had always been good with my hands and after my accident, with some study and by apprenticing myself to a good master, learned to be a cobbler.

I was able to keep body and soul together in this trade, as Portsmouth is a populous place, with sailors forever coming and going and needing their boots mended. I even did well enough to help the youngsters I saw haunting the streets, especially in the evenings. For the lads it is being idle that makes them prey to those who would use them and abuse them. The girls are even more vulnerable, as you may well imagine. I thought that with a little education they might be able to do as I did and learn an honest trade. So my little Ragged School (as it has been called these last years, I did not make up the name myself) was born.

My girls and boys (sometimes as many as forty!) come to me of an evening. Most of them are engaged in trying to earn a few pence each day, even if it is for the boys only diving from the walls of our Sally Port to retrieve coppers thrown in the water by people who enjoy the sport, and for the girls helping to hang out the wash in the yards. They sit around on the benches or the floor, and I talk to them about what learning can help them achieve. In the beginning I used to keep hot potatoes in the pockets I had sewn into my coat and go into the poor parts of town to give them to the youngsters, telling them there was more back in my workshop. Of course, they came for the food, but they stayed and they learned. Those who know something teach those who know nothing, and so it goes on. I have been doing it about thirty years now and I hope to continue until I die.

In answer to your question, I should say that Bible stories have, of course, been good reading for my youngsters, but I also use story books, newspapers, or any printed material they might enjoy. Then, too, when I can, I take them out of the city up onto Portsdown Hill. You may know that the city of Portsmouth lies between the Southdowns at its back and the Solent at its front. The views obtained from the top of Portsdown Hill are marvelous to behold and give the children a sense of geography that they have never experienced. Since the Downs are covered in furze and bushes, home to animals of every sort, the children can enjoy simple nature, and it does them as much good as any book learning.

I wish you all good luck. I do not think I am in any way able to make the trip to London, but if you should like to see me and my group you are most welcome here in Portsmouth.

I am, Madam, your most obedient servant,
John Pounds, Cobbler.

Cecilia was inspired by this letter, and determined that, if she could, she would visit John Pounds. She was delighted to see that he used a variety of materials to teach reading. Many old-fashioned educators still believed that only the Bible was appropriate for the formation of young minds. But she had seen how the story of Dick Whittington had encouraged Bridget, dealing as it does, before Dick goes on his travels, with places and things they were familiar with and then with foreign places from which they could learn that not all people are alike. She replied to Mr. Pounds that she would make every effort to visit him and began to wonder how the journey to Portsmouth would be best achieved. There would be no question of her taking her uncle's carriage, she was sure.

The second letter was markedly different.

Broome House, London

My dear Cecilia,

I have now spoken of our betrothal to my grandmother, the Dowager Lady Ianthe Broome. I had a fearful time directing her focus from my favorite waistcoat, of which she has always been the most outspoken critic. I should perhaps have chosen another, but I had rather hoped that the news of my betrothal might so relieve her mind of what has been (it seems to me) her chief preoccupation for some time, that her severe opinion of my raiment, openly and frequently expressed, might be tempered. It was not to be.

No sooner had I arrived than she required me to remove myself from her sight lest I damage her eyesight. I found this excessive, and told her so. Her own husband, my late and not very regretted grandfather, was well known for disporting himself in garments of far greater luminosity than mine. He was fond of mirrors and sequins. Need I say more? Nonetheless, it has always been (to my intense chagrin) that what she deplores in my appearance she was blind to in that of her late lord. It could be that the effulgence of his person did indeed affect her eyesight and that she now sees as if through a veil of some sort. When I pointed this out to her, her response was such that I dare not, for propriety's sake, repeat here.

We did at length put down the cudgels long enough for me to inform her of our betrothal, which, mirabile dictu, *she refused to believe! After having pushed me towards marriage for these three years at least, she now claims that no woman of any sense would agree to affiance herself with someone whose jib, she says, is cut in a way of which no reasonable girl could possibly approve. In short, she says she will only believe it if she hears it from your lips and without my presence. Accordingly, I am forced to put you to the trial of a tête à tête with this formidable grand dame.*

I fear I may vex you with my next remarks and I hope you will take it as proof of my stoutness of heart that I nonetheless make them. It will not surprise you to learn that my grandmother, though she deplores my sartorial choices, and she would say because of it, is a lady of decided fashion. For her to see you in your drab grey would be an embarrassment for both of you. I have therefore taken the liberty of making an appointment for you at a discreet modiste well known to me who will, as a matter of urgency, provide you with new apparel. I can see you, Cecilia, looking at me in that delightfully haughty way you have, but I must beg you to accept this as a betrothal gift. I have mendaciously informed my grandmother that you are presently from home, visiting an aged retainer. She is expecting you for tea next week. I shall send a carriage to convey you to her house. The appointments and directions are shown overleaf.

In view of these developments, I fear that the announcement of our betrothal must be at the end of next week, not this. But I must now repair to my tailor, for once it is known, I shall myself be expected to appear in something new. I am considering ruby red with gold braid, which seems suitably solemn, but with a hint of military whimsy. What do you think?

Please accept, my dear Cecilia, the expression of my most sincere admiration. You will note I make no mention of respect or affection, though I assure you of both.

Yours,
Tommy

He was right that she found the idea of his buying her a gown intolerable, and she would have liked to refuse absolutely. But she knew that her old grey gowns were as unbecoming as Tommy had said. After nibbling the end of her pen thoughtfully, she wrote thanking him for his forethought. She wasn't sure what he meant by her *delightfully haughty* manner but told him that she would most certainly pay the modiste herself. Finally, she said she thought ruby red with gold would become him admirably, so long as it were not puce.

While their niece was thus engaged, Lord and Lady Beaumaris were shaking their heads at her folly.

"M'brother was not altogether sensible, you remember. I wonder if she doesn't have it from him. He used to imagine things."

"Your brother was a fool!" replied his wife unequivocally. "Always had his head stuck in a book and never saw anything further than the end of his nose."

They both sighed. "Poor girl!" said Lady Beaumaris.

Chapter Eight

It came as no surprise to the very few who had been informed of the betrothal that no notice appeared in any newspaper that week. Cecilia's aunt and uncle simply shook their heads sorrowfully over the self-deception of their niece, wondering if they should call for the doctor. The Dowager Countess, supremely confident that Tommy would do nothing without her approval, expected none. She would have been astonished to learn that her wayward grandson was going to do exactly what he pleased, and the absence of a notice in the papers was due to the lack of a suitable wardrobe for Cecilia, which concerned him very much, rather than the lack of his grandmother's approval, which concerned him not at all.

The day after her receipt of Tommy's letter saw Cecilia entering the doors of a very select establishment, where she was greeted with great deference and shown into an elegant room surrounded by mirrors. There, she was gently undressed down to her chemise and, supervised by Madame Clothilde, measured in every imaginable way. She was then put into a silk wrapper and asked to take the pins out of her hair. While she enjoyed a cup of tea, the minions of the establishment brought in rolls of silk, brocade and fine wool in various hues of the colors Tommy had recommended. As she sat in front of the mirrors, the different materials were brought up to her face and hair as Madame said *yes*, or *no* or sometimes *perhaps* with bewildering rapidity in a voice that brooked no dispute. Then several large folios of models were laid before her. At first, Cecilia timidly attempted to indicate which ones she preferred, but in nearly every case, her choice was overridden by the modiste whose raised eyebrows quickly reduced her to silence.

"My dear Miss Beaumaris," said that lady finally. "I think you are too much influenced by what you see other ladies wearing. If I may say it, you are not like other ladies and your style must be your own. You simply may not wear anything with rosebuds all over the front, or lace over the shoulders, or ruffled down the skirt. Your tall figure must be allowed to speak for itself. Of prime importance must be the cut. Your gowns must fit you impeccably. It is fortunate that the fashion for perfectly straight gowns falling from the bodice is now waning, since with your height and generous bosom, it cannot be regarded as altogether suitable for you. Your day gowns must be cut to follow your shape, without fullness in the skirts. They must emphasize your regal neck and head. I think a somewhat military look with a braid-edged stand-up collar in the back, a row of braiding under the bosom and around the bottom of the skirt would be admirable. The moss green would be an excellent choice. For evening gowns, they must be cut lower, of course, and with your height you must wear a longer length train or even a wide flounce around the underdress. The yellow gold or amber would be admirable. On no account must you wear floral crowns in your hair! Tall plumes are for you!

"But, Madame, I am already tall enough!"

"Exactly. Imagine tall plumes on a short lady. Ridiculous!" Then, relenting a little, "My dear Miss Beaumaris, if I may say, you are not a pretty little thing. You are, or could be, beautiful. You must not try to hide your attributes. Accentuate them! You are tall. Make yourself taller! You have a generous bosom. Display it, tastefully, of course. You are larger than other ladies, but you are slim. Do not cover yourself with frills and furbelows in an attempt to look smaller. Lord Tommy told me how you are and he is exactly right. Of course, his taste is unerring. Whenever he has ordered a gown for ... for," she hesitated, reluctant to use the words that came to her tongue, "for his *friends*, he has always known better than they what becomes them. I cannot tell you the disputes I have had with them, but he was always right."

"Very well," sighed Cecilia, preferring not to investigate who these *friends* might be, "I shall be guided by you, Madame. You must know from my appearance when I arrived that I am not in the habit of dressing myself for fashion. But I must have a gown for ... for a special purpose, and I am grateful to you for taking this on at such short notice. I would be pleased to take your account today, if I may. I shall ask my man of business to send you a draft."

"Oh, my dear, there will be time to talk of accounts and drafts when the gowns ... I mean *gown* is made. Delivery will be next Tuesday. With your permission, I shall accompany the ... *it*, to make sure the fit is satisfactory."

Cecilia noticed the hesitation in the modiste's voice, but put it down to the pressure of completing her order in such a short time.

The weekend passed quietly. Cecilia sent her apologies to a party she had been invited to on the Saturday evening and instead spent time at the kitchen table with her pupils. Bridget could by now read nearly the whole of Dick Whittington and her dictionary covered several pages. Rose, the other scullery maid, was making slower progress, and was inclined to make wild guesses as to the words she was trying to read, much to her friend's scorn.

"'Ow can you fink that says *mouse* when you can see it don't begin with no M. Look it's an R. Wot do yer fink?"

"Rat?" said Rose. "Could be *rat*."

"Course it is, you wet. It even begins wiv the same letter as yer name: Rose. Honest, I don't know wot yer finkin'."

Cecilia had to smile at her young friend's teaching method. But it seemed to work, for Rose was learning.

On Sunday morning she went quietly to church. Her aunt and uncle were convinced that she was down in the mouth from her obvious disappointment. They even wondered whether she might be considering joining a cloister.

On Monday afternoon a carriage drew up and a footman delivered a large bandbox addressed to Miss Beaumaris. The carriage bore a crest showing a shield divided vertically through the center with the heads of three horses on the left section, which was blue, and three gold crescent moons on a white background on the right. The name Broome appeared beneath in gold. Much intrigued, she took the bandbox up to her room and there uncovered a beautiful high poke bonnet with a note:

> *Dear Cecilia,. This should go with whichever gown you wear. Recommend the ribbon by your ear.*
> *Tommy.*

Whatever did he mean, *whichever gown*? But she gave it no more thought as, with most uncharacteristic enthusiasm, she placed the bonnet on her head. It was of a fine pale tan felt; the underside of the poke was covered in pleated amber silk. Feathers in green, amber and gold curled on one side towards her face. As directed by her betrothed, she tied the ribbons, the same pale tan as the bonnet, by the ear opposite the feathers, and stood back to take in the effect. A stranger looked back at her in the mirror. Her dark curls, pushed forward by the bonnet, framed her face, glowing next to the feathers that fell from the high crown. Her eyes reflected the gold and amber. It was the most becoming thing she had ever put on her head. For the rest of the day, she chided herself for her impatience to see her new gown on the morrow.

Cecilia's aunt had been out when the crested carriage had arrived the day before, but when it came on the Tuesday, bearing Madame Clothilde, an acolyte, and a large number of band boxes, she witnessed it through the tall front windows that gave onto Bruton Street. She waited for the butler to announce the visitor, but when time passed and no one entered the drawing room, she forsook her habitual indolence and pulled the bell.

"The … female arrived for Miss Beaumaris," he answered when questioned, his hesitation in describing the visitor conveying immediately to his mistress that, while the person in question was not a lady, she was the sort one might allow to enter the house. "I … er I took her to be a dressmaker, my lady. They are now upstairs in Miss Beaumaris's bedchamber."

Weak in the knees her ladyship might be, but the speed with which she mounted the stairs showed that when she wanted to, she had all the capacity to do so. She knocked on Cecilia's door and entered, to find a number of open boxes, a profusion of tissue paper and an array of garments lying on the bed and the chairs. Her niece was standing in the middle with a look of dismay on her face.

"Aunt!" exclaimed Cecilia, "There has been some sort of mistake. I ordered a gown from Madame Clothilde last week, but *seven* have been delivered."

Lady Beaumaris at once recognized the name of the most exclusive modiste in London, and one she herself she could never afford.

The dressmaker curtseyed and said, in a soothing but professional tone, "There is no mistake. These gowns have been ordered and paid for, together with a pelisse, a pair of kid gloves and shoes. All that remains is for Miss Beaumaris to try them on and make sure there has been no error in the making of them. Since I oversaw the whole myself, I very much doubt it."

"But who paid for them?" her ladyship blurted out before she could stop herself.

"Miss Beaumaris's fiancé. He informed me the apparel was by way of a betrothal gift."

"Tommy!" exclaimed Cecilia, at the same time as her aunt cried "Fiancé?" in a tone of utter disbelief.

"I told him I wanted to pay for my own gown!" Cecilia looked frantically from one to the other. "How was I to know he had arranged all this?"

"His lordship did mention that it might be something of a shock," replied the modiste calmly, "but asked me to tell you that he was sorry, but could not help himself. 'Carried away' were the words he used. He is, as you know, something of an expert in ladies' apparel."

Cecilia sat down on her bed, but quickly arose, since she was crushing a shimmering gold ballgown, complete with ostrich feathers.

"But I can't take all this!" she cried in dismay. "The betrothal is only ... only ..." Words failed her, as she knew she could not say what she meant: that the betrothal was a sham, not real, a fake.

After the initial shock, Lady Beaumaris had realized that Cecilia's announcement after the weekend had not, after all, been the product of a fevered imagination. Her breast swelled with pride to think that she would soon be related to one of the richest and most sought-after men in the country.

"Of course, my dear," she said soothingly, "you mean the betrothal is only of a recent date and not yet generally known, but I am sure that when it is, you will have need of all these," she gestured around the littered bedroom floor. "There will be family gatherings, teas, balls ... a host of things. You have no idea!"

Cecilia suddenly knew that what she said was true. She inwardly cursed herself for not thinking of that aspect of things. She had agreed to the betrothal because she wanted peace, a relief from the constant unwanted attention of fortune hunters. Now she was to be precipitated into an even more oppressive social round. She looked around her and sighed. She would have to make the best of the situation for the time being. It would not be seemly to argue with the modiste, and the less discussion with her aunt, the better. She would write to Tommy.

"Very well," she said, more calmly than she felt. "I had best try on all this ... finery. I don't want his lordship to feel he has wasted his money. If you will excuse me, aunt."

Reluctantly, her aunt left the bedchamber. The next hour was a revelation to Cecilia. Generally speaking, if clients did not come with a pattern in mind, dressmakers would either have one of their assistants model the latest styles or have standard size gowns for clients to try on. Then a gown would be made to measure. Cecilia had never had the luxury of being able to try on a gown that fit her anywhere. Here, there were seven: two fine wool day dresses in moss green and lilac, two silk evening dresses in amber and sapphire blue, two ball gowns, the gold satin one she had sat upon and one in shot blue taffeta with an elusive green light, and a wool walking outfit in bottle green with a thin black herringbone pattern.

They all fit her to perfection. They were long enough, a miracle in itself; the sleeves actually came to her wrist instead of half way up her arm. They all fit across the shoulders and were long enough in the waist. Above all, they were so comfortable! Since reaching her full height she had never been able to find a gown that was not uncomfortable somewhere, pulling across the chest or under the arms. That is why she had taken to wearing loose styles that did not constrict anywhere. Now she saw what a well-tailored gown did for her figure. She had put on the moss green gown with the stand-up collar and braid. Instead of looking large and lumpish, she looked slender and elegant. The color enhanced the gold-brown of her eyes and the glow in her dark hair.

"There, Madam!" said the modiste with great satisfaction. "Was I not right that this style would become you admirably? I told Lord Tommy – you will forgive me, that is what we always call him – what we had decided, and he was in perfect agreement. He instructed me to make up all the gowns. Did I not tell you his taste is unerring?"

Cecilia tried on all the other gowns as well as the new pelisse, gloves, and shoes. She had wondered why they had measured her hands and feet, now she knew. Madame Clothilde was right.

Tommy's taste was perfect. She smiled at the thought of him in his blue coat and his exhortations not to wrinkle his sleeves when they waltzed.

Two days later at just before three in the afternoon, the crested carriage stopped once again in front of the house in Bruton Street. A groom put the steps down for Cecilia and handed her in. She had come downstairs at the last minute, having asked the butler to call her when he saw the carriage approaching. She had not wanted to engage in any more probing conversations with her aunt and uncle. The previous two days had been a trial. Her uncle had tried in his ponderous way to joke with her about her cunning entrapment of the *ton's* most sought-after bachelor, encouraged by her aunt's arch interrogation about exactly how she had been able to pursue an acquaintance with the Earl. Not being able to tell them about their disagreement over dinner, nor about the strange meeting in the library, she was obliged to be vague. They were clearly dissatisfied and repeatedly asked her the same questions. She could not sit at table or spend any time in the drawing room without the subject being raised again and again. She spent as much time as she could in her room.

Now she was ensconced in the Earl's carriage, having refused the groom's offer of a rug over her knees, conscious that she was looking better than she had ever looked in her life. She was wearing the moss green gown with her new pelisse and bonnet, and her reflection in the bedroom mirror showed an elegant woman she hardly recognized as herself. She had long ago schooled herself to keep her nerves in check – only small women could claim to be subject to nerves – but she had to admit that she was not looking forward to the interview with her betrothed's grandmother. He had described her as formidable, and Cecilia had a mental image of a hook-nosed matron, along the lines of Lady March.

She was therefore astonished, when the butler announced her into the presence of the Dowager Countess of Broome, to find herself confronting a very pretty, petite lady who appeared, at first sight, to be no more than forty. She was sitting in a feminine drawing room which seemed suffused with a pink light. She realized it was because, while a many-branched chandelier stood some yards behind her ladyship, filmy curtains of a pinkish hue covered the windows. The Dowager, who would herself never use the term, as she despised the sense of age it automatically bestowed, rose, beckoned her forward and begged her to sit. Closer up, Cecilia could see that the youthfulness of her hostess had not been achieved entirely without assistance. Her make-up, while so skillful as to be all but invisible, could not disguise the lines around her eyes or down the sides of her mouth, and the pretty gold of her curls, peeping from beneath a fetching lace cap, must, in Cecilia's opinion, have owed more to a bottle than to nature. But the whole effect was of a lovely lady in her middle years. Her ladyship looked as fragile as a Dresden doll. Cecilia wondered how Tommy could find her formidable.

For her part, the Countess had to stifle an expression of shock when an Amazon, admirably dressed in the height of fashion, came forward to greet her. She stood to meet her grandson's fiancée and had to look up into her face. She took in the dark curls and a high feathered bonnet she would not have despised to wear herself, had she had the necessary inches. She admired the calm expression in the dark, gold flecked eyes, the regal bearing and the beautiful tailoring of her gown. So this was Miss Beaumaris! She certainly looked like an heiress. But more than that, she looked like a woman who knew her own mind. Whatever, thought the Countess, had made her accept Tommy?

While the tray was being brought in and the tea served, the Countess kept up a flow of small talk that would have put a girl with much less self-assurance than Cecilia at her ease. She contributed calmly in her pleasant low voice, showing herself neither distant nor overly eager to please. They covered the mildness of the October weather, the beauties of the countryside around Highmount, the latest play at the Theatre Royal, which Cecilia freely admitted she had not seen. Finally, when the butler and footmen had withdrawn, the Dowager went on the attack.

"When I mentioned your name to my grandson before his trip to Highmount, he did not indicate he knew you, Miss Beaumaris," she observed lightly, but with a glint in her eye.

"We were not acquainted before that weekend, my lady," responded Cecilia calmly, but uncomfortable with where she could see this was leading.

"So it was a case of love at first sight! How romantic! I must say, I would never have thought it of Tommy," came the response.

"It was …" Cecilia thought furiously, "it was a fortunate meeting for both of us."

"Fortunate?"

"Yes, we … we quickly found we had things in common."

"What things?" Her ladyship swooped in like an eagle on a mouse.

"A … a dislike of certain types of society."

"I'm not sure I understand you. What society?"

"Persons who importune one, demanding individuals."

"And I'm to understand you found my grandson not of that number?"

"Yes."

The Countess thought for a moment.

"Tell me plainly, Miss Beaumaris. Why did you accept Tommy?"

"He…" Cecilia did not know how to answer. *Because he suggested a false betrothal to save us both from those who try to make us do things we don't like, including yourself, my lady?* She could hardly say that. "Because he is kind and … he makes me laugh." That, at least, was true.

If the Countess thought this an odd answer, she said nothing but changed tack. "You will forgive my bluntness, Miss Beaumaris, but Tommy is my only grandson and the head of an important family. His parents are deceased. Until today you have been unknown to me. I want to know you better. I understand you are an heiress, Miss Beaumaris?"

"I am not an heiress. My father was the younger son of the late Lord Beaumaris. He inherited a competence. My mother was a Wincanton. She had a little money of her own. What little was left of both came to me when they died."

Cecilia did not want to rehearse the whole of her childhood with this lady and her penetrating questions. She and Tommy had never discussed money, nor were ever likely to. It was no one's business but her own.

"I see." In fact, the Dowager did not see. Miss Beaumaris's bonnet and gown were not the apparel of someone with a mere competence. "You must know," she continued, "that Tommy is a very wealthy man, besides what he will inherit from me. I imagine this has been one of the causes of the ... importuning he has had to suffer. Most young women will not say no to a fortune, especially when it is attached to a man as personable as my grandson, in spite of his ... peculiarities."

"I assure you, Madam," replied Cecilia with some heat, "that consideration of your grandson's fortune was the absolutely last thing on my mind when I entered into this ... this betrothal. I neither need nor want his money."

The Dowager Lady Broome opened her eyes very wide at this declaration and would have answered except that at that moment a voice known to both of them was heard in the hall.

"Afternoon, Mobley. Miss Beaumaris still with her ladyship? Good. Don't bother to announce me, I know the way!"

And Tommy came in, resplendent in a beautifully tailored light grey coat over yellow pantaloons that fit without a single wrinkle, Hessians that could have been used as a mirror, a grey and yellow checked waistcoat and a neckcloth, so white that it shone in the dim light and in such a nicety of folds that it looked molded to his neck. He took one look at Cecilia and his eyebrows rose and his eyes danced with pleasure. He came forward, bowed over her hand, and then went to his grandmother.

"Hello Gran!" he said, "Came to stop you grillin' my poor Cecilia the way you grill me."

"I have told you not to call me by that low name, Thomas!" remonstrated his grandmother. "And what can you mean? Miss

Beaumaris and I are having a nice cose. You are not welcome to join us."

Since her interview was becoming the least delightful cose Cecilia had ever had in her life, she had never been as pleased to see anyone as she was to see Tommy, and there was no denying the words *my Cecilia* warmed her heart. She gave him a wholehearted smile that was not lost on her hostess.

"Well, no doubt you are pleased to see him, Miss Beaumaris," she said, "though why you should have accepted such a popinjay is still a mystery to me. I'm glad he makes you laugh, for I must confess that the only emotion he arouses in my breast is the desire to weep!"

"Now Gran, you know that ain't true! You smiled only last week at something I told you. Can't remember what it was, probably something to the discredit of one of the old tabbies you say are your friends. That always cheers you up!"

He pulled a bergère chair over next to Cecilia and took her hand.

"That's a mighty fetchin' gown you're wearin'," he said. "Is it new? Never saw you look better, my dear."

Cecilia blushed and did not know quite what to say. But her ladyship agreed.

"Yes. Miss Beaumaris's gown and bonnet make me quite envious. Not that I could wear anything like that, of course, I should look a positive antidote. You could learn a thing or two from her, Tommy, about what is becoming and what is not. Though you look very nice today," she said, relenting.

"Well, grandmother, now we've established that you think we both look quite presentable, which Miss Beaumaris's case is nothing extraordinary, but in mine is a rare and wonderful occurrence, I'm going to get old Mobley to bring up some of that champagne I know my father had you put down back in '95."

He went out of the room and could be heard talking to the butler. Lady Broome looked at her.

"He is a ridiculous boy, but he is the light of my old age," she said seriously. I pray you, dear Miss Beaumaris, don't break his heart. I believe it when you say his fortune isn't a consideration with you. I confess I don't quite understand it all, but I trust you will make him happy."

Nothing could have been more designed to make Cecilia conscious of her perfidy. She very nearly confessed the truth, but his lordship chose that moment to return and in a few minutes Mobley came in with champagne and pink biscuits. With Tommy acting a complete fool, attempting to drink champagne out of her shoe, and Cecilia laughingly remonstrating with him, the rest of the visit passed off in great good humor.

The Dowager Lady Broome looked fondly from the one to the other. To be sure, Miss Beaumaris was nothing like the girls she had thrown in Tommy's path over the last three years, but she had to admit she liked her. More than that, she respected her. She had the sense that there was more to her grandson's betrothed than met the eye, although what met the eye was by no means to be dismissed. When they stood to leave, she thought what a handsome couple they made, he so fair and she so dark, with her high poke bonnet making her as tall as he, or even a shade taller, smiling at each other in obvious good humor.

Tommy accompanied her home in the carriage and Cecilia tried to bring up the vexing question of his having paid for her new wardrobe. But she found it impossible to make him understand that she could not accept such a lavish gift.

"My dear Cecilia," he said solemnly, "Please do not destroy for me the pleasure I have derived from seeing you properly attired. You cannot be so cruel as to take that from me. Please do not talk about it anymore. It is a dagger in my heart."

Saying that the following day would see the notice in the newspaper and that he would collect her for a ball to which they had both been invited, he kissed her hand and left her in Bruton Street.

Chapter Nine

The betrothal is announced, ran the notice in all the newspapers the following day, *of Cecilia Anne Beaumaris, only daughter of the late Honorable William Beaumaris, and his wife Anne (née Wincanton), and the Lord Thomas Algernon Wymering Allenby, fourth Earl of Broome.*

No other information was forthcoming, nor any needed, to throw the *ton* into a fever of gossip and conjecture. A few of the people who had been at Highmount nodded sagely and said they were not surprised. Tommy had shown a distinct inclination for Cecilia Beaumaris over the weekend, though why, heaven knew, since she had no address and was much too tall for beauty. The young women who had treasured hopes of the Earl were inclined to think it was a mistake. He had never been known to pay court to anyone like her. Their mothers, who dimly remembered Cecilia's parents, said they had always been an odd family and ten to one it was some sort of joke, which would be just like young Thomas. It was not until the ball on the Saturday night that the notice was shown to be nothing short of the truth.

As promised, Tommy called for Cecilia in Bruton Street and as soon as they were in the carriage, he took a small box from his pocket and gave it to her.

"Thought you'd better have one of these," he said. "Not family jewels, of course, just to satisfy the old tabbies. Bound to look at your finger, you see."

Cecilia opened the box to see a ring with a large square cut emerald surrounded by diamonds. It was lovely. She drew in her breath and, half wishing this were not happening, and half filled with a desire to see the lovely ring on her hand, she could not stop herself from taking it out of the box. She held it up, the stones catching the flare from the gaslights that lined the London streets. When it came to it, though, she was entirely unable to put it on the fourth finger of her left hand. Seeing her hesitation, Tommy took the ring from her and placed it there himself. It slid on and lay against her finger, an absolutely perfect size both for the finger and for her hand.

"Knew that size and the square cut would be just the thing," said Tommy, with satisfaction. "Had the measurements from Clothilde."

"But Tommy… I can't … you can't …" stammered Cecilia. "I never thought …"

"Can't be betrothed without a ring," said Tommy matter-of-factly. "People would smell a rat. Anyway, I want you to have it. No one else could wear it."

Cecilia looked at him. "It's beautiful, Tommy. The most beautiful thing anyone has ever given me, thank you. But really, honestly, you must stop buying me things. What shall I do at the end, when it's all called off? I feel dreadful acting under false pretenses like this. If I'd thought it through, I never would have accepted, and I'm convinced if you had thought about it more, you would never have suggested it either."

"Nonsense. Never had so much fun in m'life as choosing those gowns for you. Felt like that Greek chap Gally something. Made a statue and she came to life. Not that you're made of marble, but well, you know. You weren't really alive, wearin' all that rubbish. I brought you to life. And I told you, the ring's not family stuff. It's yours to keep. Don't want it back. Wouldn't fit anyone else, anyway."

"You mean Pygmalion," said Cecilia, ever the teacher. "The woman he created was called Galatea and she was his ideal. No one could ever call me that, though I thank you for the compliment." She smiled at him.

"Don't know about that. In that gown with the plumes in your hair you look like a queen and I've always had a taste for royalty," said Tommy, smiling back.

Cecilia had put on the gold gown she had so nearly crushed and, with great misgivings, had clipped the plumes to the side of her head. Her curls were caught up on top, with ringlets framing her face. She wore no earrings or necklace, thinking the plumes quite enough. Besides, all she had were her mother's pearl earrings and a locket with her parents' likenesses inside, and neither seemed appropriate. She owned no evening cloak, but the weather remained mild for the time of year, so she had simply brought the shawl her aunt had given her. As she had come down the stairs in Bruton Street, her uncle had lifted his eye glass with astonishment and her aunt had let out a long breath.

"My dear, you look magnificent," she breathed. "I swear I would not have known you. I wish your mother could see you now."

Since Cecilia's mother had been a stern critic of feminine furbelows and had worn nothing but the shapeless grey gowns that were the model for her own attire until a week ago, she was not sure if her appearance would have met with that ascetic woman's approval. She would most certainly have deplored the plumes, which Cecilia had to admit, were, quite literally, the height of folly. They brushed the ceiling of the coach in which they now sat.

Tommy had gone ahead with the ruby red coat he had written about in his letter. It was in silk satin, with wide cut-away lapels edged in gold braid. His waistcoat and britches were white, as customary for a ball. His neckcloth was, as usual, arranged in intricate folds and tonight held with a ruby-headed pin. It should have been ridiculous, but he looked perfect. When they arrived at the Mayfair *hôtel particulier* where the ball was to be held, and Tommy handed her down from the carriage, there was something about his bearing that made her stand up even straighter and bear the plumes proudly as they mounted the steps to the front door.

When they were announced, there was a momentary hush and the whole assembly turned to look at Lord Tommy and his betrothed. Many of them had never seen her before, and even those who had scarcely recognized her. They looked spectacular together, the plumes on her lustrous dark head rising above his shining curls, the gold of her magnificent gown mirrored in the braid of his coat; they seemed of a different, superior breed. Some of the younger and less experienced in the crowd felt an instinctive move to bow and curtsey, as if to royalty.

For Cecilia, the evening was a revelation. She was never allowed to stand on the fringes as she usually did. People flocked to them both and she was included in their greetings, their congratulations, their conversations. For the first time in her life, she felt as if she belonged.

She saw the women look enviously at her gown and her ring and the men at her décolletage. She had never worn gowns in any way revealing before and had wondered if she would be able to carry it off. But the cut that Madame Clothilde had achieved was a masterpiece. In reality it covered more than it exposed, while hinting at the fullness beneath. The gentlemen's appreciative glances were entirely new to her, and though she scolded herself for being so shallow, she found she enjoyed it. Tommy was the perfect escort, never pushing her forward nor overshadowing her. She was entertained by his endless flow of conversation, much of it very silly. She found herself laughing with him and as a result, in good humor with the rest of the world.

Amongst the other guests at the ball was a vivacious young woman of about Cecilia's age who Tommy pointed out as his younger sister, Mariah. He explained that his older sister, Eugenia, was wife to the Ambassador in Vienna and consequently not in London.

"Very grand," he said, "Will be just like grandmother in a couple of years. Already constantly writin' to tell me my duty."

Mariah, however, had been married just the year before to the Baron Chesterford, a nice-looking man in his early thirties. They seemed a devoted couple and were talking head to head, oblivious of everyone else.

"Chesterford's rolled-up, of course," said Tommy as he was ushering her towards the couple. "Not a feather to fly with, but Mariah's got a nice little fortune and they deal very well together. It was a love match. M'grandmother and Eugenia were none too keen. Thought he was a fortune hunter. But, truth is, he never looked at another girl once he'd met m'sister and she's mighty fond of him. Look at 'em canoodling. Shockin', ain't it?"

"Evenin' sister mine," said Tommy when they were standing in front of the young couple, "and to you, Chesterford. Want to present my betrothed, Cecilia Beaumaris: Lord Hugo and Lady Mariah Chesterford."

They exchanged bows and curtseys, and then Mariah exclaimed in what Cecilia was to come to recognize as her habitual exuberant fashion, "Oh good! I was hoping I'd see you here, Cecilia – I may call you that, mayn't I, we are to be sisters after all," but before Cecilia could even nod assent, went on, "We all saw the notice in the papers and thought at first it was just Tommy up to his tricks, but someone saw Grandmother who assured us it was true. Just like you, Tommy, not to even hint to anyone in the family you was going to propose! I must say, I thought it pretty shabby! I suppose you'll say it was none of our business, but I told *you* when I thought Hugo was going to pop the question, didn't I, and jolly fed up you would have been if I hadn't! I must say," she continued, without drawing breath but now addressing herself to Cecilia, "you don't look a bit like any of his other … well," she hesitated, "his lady friends. Does she, Hugo? Much grander. Good thing! Hope you can keep him in line. He needs a firm hand, we all think so, even though he's the head of the family. I say Tommy, what a quiz of a coat! Jolly mean of you too, as you're always telling us not to wear pink or anything like that!"

Tommy had paid little attention to his sister's effusive speech, and was busy picking an infinitesimal piece of fluff off his waistcoat, but when she mentioned his coat he lifted his head and said, ruffled, "It is not a quiz of a coat and it is most certainly not *pink*! If you can't tell the difference between ruby and pink, no wonder every gown you propose to buy is a horror! That thing you've got on tonight is not fit to be seen in, at least, not by you! How many times do I have to tell you, no bright yellow! No bright green! No bright anything!"

It was true that Mariah was much fairer than Tommy, whose hair was guinea gold. Hers was more flaxen, and the citrus yellow gown she wore, thankfully muted by a chiffon overdress, was not entirely becoming.

"Oh, Tommy! How you do go on! You think no one can decide on anything without your guidance. Look at Cecilia! I'll wager you had nothing to do with that gorgeous gold creation, and she looks marvelous!"

Cecilia was on the point of explaining that Tommy had everything to do with it, when he responded, "I'm glad to say that my betrothed has good taste. How could it be otherwise?" he smiled at her. "But come, Cecilia, let's leave these lovebirds together. You're a stout fellow, Chesterford, if you can bear to have her on your arm in that gown!"

To a cry of protest from Mariah and a soothing mutter from her husband, they walked away, Cecilia thinking not at all about the inadvisability of wearing citrus yellow when one is very fair, but very much about Mariah's comment concerning Tommy's previous lady friends. How many had there been, she wondered.

The musicians had struck in in preparation for the dancing. Cecilia had the new experience of having her dance card filled to the point where she had to refuse some gentlemen, even at one point, Tommy. Her betrothed reacted with outrage.

"'Pon my soul, Cecilia, it's a fine thing when a man cannot get a dance with his own fiancée! Let's see!" He took the dance card from her hand and ruthlessly scratched out a number of entries. "Old Pip – Philip Turner – get rid of him; Tommy Fairbrother?

Certainly not! What's this awful scrawl? Can't even read it. Oh, Bill Worthington! Better leave him in. Much bigger than me, handy with his fives. But Bunty Gall? Never – he's gone!"

"What do you mean, Tommy?" laughed Cecilia. "You don't mean you've scratched out the gentlemen you think you could defeat in a fight?"

"Of course! No point in picking a quarrel with a feller you know you can't take. But those three, no problem!"

"You're funning me! I don't believe you would fight anyone, certainly not over a dance!"

"Oh, I wouldn't say that," said a gentleman in hearing distance. "Got a fierce left, old Tommy! I wouldn't like to take him on!"

Whether it was because of his fierce left, or simply because the three gentlemen in question accepted Tommy's superior claim, Cecilia was left to dance three times with her betrothed and did not sit out once all evening. At last, after a supper of white soup and asparagus spears in pastry cases, Tommy took her home.

"M' sister was right. You look absolutely stunning tonight my dear," he said as they rolled along in the carriage.

"Thanks to you, Tommy," replied Cecilia with a smile. "I would never have chosen anything like this for myself. You are a marvel! And you were right about your ruby red coat. It looks wonderful on you, though I can't imagine anyone else being able to carry it off."

He kissed her hand and handed her out of the carriage in Bruton Street. "A perfect couple, in fact," he said, and bowed good night.

Over the next couple of months, the perfect couple was seen together at numerous parties, routs and at least two other balls. If Cecilia did not get the peace and quiet she had been hoping for, she did learn that an evening spent with someone whom you liked and who made you laugh was very pleasurable indeed. She tried to chide herself for enjoying such dissipation, but ended up simply thinking that she would need to order more evening dresses and another ball gown. However, she would need to see what her finances really were before engaging in such purchases. She was determined not to let Tommy pay for anything else. He had already bought her a sumptuous black velvet cloak lined with mink. The fur also appeared in a wide band around the cuffs, the hood and the hem. When she protested that she could not possibly accept anything so costly, he responded that she would be doing him a favor. It was perfect for her: a cloak with such wide bands of fur could only be worn by a tall woman, so that if he were forced to see anyone else wear it, it would bring tears to his eyes.

"Truly, Tommy," she pleaded, "Be serious! You know this will all be over in a few months, and I shall have no use for a mink lined evening cloak in the East End! I cannot continue to accept such gifts from you."

"Don't refine so much upon it, my dear," he replied. "I'm as rich as a nabob with nothing to spend my money on. You cannot conceive what joy it gives me to have someone to buy for, especially a thing like this cloak that no one but you could wear without looking like a bear escaped from the zoo. Please don't scold me. It quite undoes all my pleasure! Anyway, I daresay those old houses in the East End are drafty and cold. You will need it to keep you warm."

After that, what could she say? Nevertheless, she was not going to mention any new gowns to her betrothed. Heaven knows what he would have Madame Clothilde make for her. Accordingly, she sent a note to Mr. William Davis in the City asking him to call on her at his earliest convenience to discuss her inheritance.

Mr. Davis turned out to be much younger than she had anticipated, since he had been her parents' man of business and she had been receiving letters from him the last fifteen years at least. He was a stocky man in his early thirties whose sparse sandy hair was combed back over an already balding pate. Nevertheless, he had a twinkle in his eye, and never more so than when she exclaimed her surprise at his not being much older.

"Ah! You are referring to my father, Miss Beaumaris. Same name, same profession. He's still in the office and overlooks things, but he doesn't like to stir out much these days. I'm his man on the street, as it were. Now, you were wanting to know about your inheritance. Let me show you."

And he laid before her a number of documents that he drew from a large heavy marbled card folder held together with brown twill ribbon. It became clear that Mr. Davis Senior had handled her inheritance with careful conservatism. While the value had dropped somewhat during these troubled times with Bonaparte, the government bonds in which it was invested had yielded an average of three percent per annum. To be sure, this was not an exciting figure, and Cecilia had the distinct impression that had it been he, and not his father, handling the business, Mr. Davis considered he might have found more lucrative investments.

"My father begged leave to tell you that your parents left you the modest sum of a little over ten thousand pounds," said Mr. Davis Junior. "They were not of a... a prudent disposition, one might say." In fact, his father had remarked it was lucky for Miss Beaumaris that they died when they did, or there would have been nothing left. "But, since you have not touched it since the payment of your school fees ended, the effect of interest means it is now worth just under fifteen thousand pounds."

"Well, that is certainly not nothing," said Cecilia, to whom such a sum sounded quite grand. "May I assume then, that if instead of reinvesting the interest every year, I took it for living expenses, I could receive about four hundred and fifty pounds a year, that being three percent of fifteen, without touching the principal?"

Mr. Davies was impressed with this demonstration of such a ready grasp of figures. "Yes, indeed, Miss Beaumaris. But bear in mind that you are young still, and that figure will not be worth as much in, say, ten years, as it is now."

"Then I might be obliged to break into the principal. But as I do not have, nor expect to have, any heirs, that can hardly matter. I need only consider my own lifetime."

"But surely, Miss Beaumaris, you are betrothed, are you not?" For Mr. Davies read the newspapers every day, and not only the financial news. "One may reasonably expect ..." his voice tailed off.

Cecilia, knowing she had betrayed herself, hardly knew how to answer. Then, thinking that only an assumption of *hauteur* could carry this off, she said grandly, "That is hardly your concern, Mr. Davis, In fact, I wish to use my own resources to open a school for poor girls in the East End. My next question is, in fact, whether you think I could rent a house there and afford to ... for two females to live in it with no additional income, on the sum I just mentioned?"

"That is a hard question to answer. I believe you may find dwellings for well under two hundred pounds a year, but not such places as would be appropriate for ... ladies. Then there is the question of servants ..." He looked around. While Lady Beaumaris might decry Bruton Street as a mediocre address, it was, nonetheless, a gentleman's residence. It had a full complement of servants, stables in the mews and horses to feed. Mr. Davis thought that if where she was living now cost less than two thousand a year to maintain, he would eat his hat. And here she was, talking about two women living on less than a quarter of that!

"I ... er, the teachers would live very simply. As for servants, I think one maid might be sufficient. Do you think it possible?"

Mr. Davis thought carefully. "Miss Beaumaris," he said finally, "It might be possible, but it would be very hard. However, I shall pursue some enquiries and let you know what I discover. Do you envision having the pupils live on the premises? One would have to consider that in determining the size of the dwelling."

"No, not really. My plan is for lessons to be in the afternoons once the working day is over. I do hope to provide a simple meal, and it is entirely possible that some of them may need shelter now and then. But I do not plan a boarding school."

"Then, if you have no other questions for me, I shall take my leave. Before I go, my father wished me to ask if you are in need of funds, in which case I would give you a draft on the bank."

"No." Cecilia made up her mind. She would not buy any more dresses, even if it meant being seen repeatedly in the old ones.

She would conserve her resources. "No," she said again, firmly. "Thank you, Mr. Davis."

Chapter Ten

The Dowager Lady Broome was closely following Cecilia's introduction into the *ton* as the fiancée of her grandson. While she herself never attended any more of the parties and balls, claiming that the crowds exhausted her and the food ruined her digestion, she had spies everywhere. These were the elderly women who still liked to appear at all the society events to which they might be invited. They were the old tabbies to whom Tommy laughingly referred, and they regularly took tea with the Dowager. Aged anywhere between fifty and seventy, though not one would ever admit to more than forty-five, gossip was their chief delight, especially if it concerned each other, or someone related to them. Nothing pleased them more than passing on an overheard comment to the detriment of another of the group, and to be gossiping about Tommy and his betrothed was bread and butter to them.

"My dear," cried Lucy Sommers, to the Dowager one afternoon over the teacups, "Miss Beaumaris is nowadays seen everywhere on Tommy's arm. A striking creature, to be sure. But I have to tell you I am puzzled about her gowns. Before she became betrothed, she was in the habit of wearing the most unbecoming dresses, and though there is something about her, so that she was always the sort of woman one would look at, no one could ever say she was well-dressed. Nowadays it is just the opposite. She is exquisitely gowned. She is positively unmissable. It may be, of course, that she is so tall, and at balls wears the tallest plumes, so one may see her over everyone's head. But on the other hand, exquisite though her gowns are, she wears the same ones, almost, one might say, in rotation.

One can only conclude that although she cast off her old shell, as it were, she has not been able to obtain many new ones."

"Indeed," replied the Dowager depressingly. "I daresay she is of the sound opinion that it is better to have two or three very good gowns than a host of inferior ones. I'm sure you will agree with that sentiment, my dear Lucy. The blue lusting you are wearing today, for example, was in its day a very good gown."

Since the Honorable Willoughby Summers had recently told his wife that the purchase of any new apparel for her was out of the question, due to a very distressing settling day at Tattersall's, she, too, was unable to either cast off her old shell or obtain a new one. She held her tongue.

But that was not the only report that Lady Broome had of her prospective granddaughter-in-law's apparently limited wardrobe and she at last determined to seek out the truth. Lady March, one of her oldest and real friends, was back in London at March House in Berkeley Square. They had come out together, and had exchanged confidences over years of married life.

Making the rare decision that an outing would do her good, the autumn weather having been so fine, she sent a note to her friend saying she would come to tea the following Thursday. Such was their friendship that peremptory announcements like this were perfectly acceptable on either side. On the day, in spite of her dresser's exhortations that at this time of the year one never knew what the weather would do, and ladies of her age should wear more than a wisp of muslin, the Dowager sallied forth looking at least twenty years younger than her actual seventy years, in a flimsy gown with nothing more than a shawl for her shoulders.

"Pooh!" she said, when her dresser tried forcing a pelisse and muff upon her. "I have never worn a pelisse before December, and not even then if I could help it. A lady does not wish to be seen bundled up as if in an old carpet! I'm not in my dotage. Get away, woman!"

The afternoon was fine, though the coachmen shook their heads over a bank of dark clouds they saw off to the east and forecast rain before the day was out. Nonetheless, the Dowager rode to her old friend's house in great high spirits, taking in on the way the changes to the streets and buildings that had occurred since her last sortie, finding none of them for the better.

The two old friends had a delightful cose, laughing at memories of their cronies when they were young and shaking their heads over the folly of their husbands thinking they could chase after lightskirts well past the age when they would be able to do anything even if they caught them.

"That's one thing I'm spared," sighed the Dowager, "Bernard was such an old fool. I vow he would have lived longer if he had kept his britches buttoned up more. But what could one do? I suppose Vernon is over all that sort of thing now?"

"Yes, well, of course, he likes to think he isn't, but the truth is that the minute dinner is over he falls asleep. The Venus de Milo herself could walk by with her shell under her arm and he wouldn't notice! But the way those girls dress these days – it's a wonder more of the men don't have an apoplexy! I declare, I saw one the other day, her petticoats so dampened and clinging to her form, she might as well have been naked!"

"I recall that pale blue chiffon you had when we were about twenty! Do you remember? I was so jealous! Bernard couldn't take his eyes off you. Honestly, when you stood with the light behind you, you could see right through it. Don't pretend you didn't know!"

"Of course I knew! But Vernon just wouldn't come up to snuff! I was expecting him to speak to Papa every day, but he never came. The day after I wore that dress, he came, though! I was engaged before teatime! Made me promise never to wear it again except when we were alone!"

They both sat, thinking about the halcyon days of their youth, until the Dowager remembered the reason for her visit.

"Talking of dresses, I don't know if you've seen Tommy's betrothed recently, but by all accounts, there's been a drastic change in her wardrobe."

"Cecilia Beaumaris? Striking girl. Funny about her and Tommy though. One minute he was asking me who she was because you'd made him come to Highmount to make her acquaintance, and the next thing is, they're engaged. He did make a point of dancing with her, but if they had any sort of understanding, neither of them said a word. Saw it in the newspaper. Never so surprised in my life! She didn't have a wardrobe that weekend, I can tell you! During the day, she wore a cut-up thing. Some sort of skirt and waistcoat. Most odd. In the evenings she had on God knows what – a grey gown of some sort, with a pretty enough shawl. But somehow, it didn't matter. I suppose because she's so tall, and good-looking in her way, she's striking no matter what she wears."

"Tommy told me about the engagement right after that weekend, said I'd ordered him to do it, so he did! Silly boy. I said I wouldn't believe it till I spoke to her, so she came to tea. She was wearing a bonnet and gown then that must have cost a pretty penny. Nice, quietly spoken girl. Lovely voice. Said she wasn't interested in Tommy's money, if you can believe it. Got quite on her high horse when I mentioned it. Says she accepted him because he made her laugh, and … something about both being tired of people who importuned them. That was the word she used. Importuned. Strange."

"I'll tell you another thing that's strange. I don't know if you remember Reverend Smythe, the chaplain at Highmount? Nice old fellow. His wife's a bit odd. Won't eat flesh. Exists on vegetables. Looks like a dried runner bean herself, if you ask me. Anyway, when I saw him after the weekend, he said he'd been talking at dinner to a Miss Beaumaris who planned, when she came into her fortune, to have her own establishment and open a school for poor girls in the East End of London. He was most impressed with her. She told him all about it. Said she'd heard about a cobbler in Portsmouth who's done much the same thing. Has Tommy said anything to you about opening a school for girls?"

"No," said the Dowager, wonderingly. "But you know Tommy, never says anything to the purpose. A school for poor girls in the East End? Doesn't sound like something he'd be interested in. Girls, yes, poor girls, no! Definitely not! Hmm …"

Shortly after this, the Dowager took her leave. It was about half past five, and when she got outside, the weather had changed. The sky was an ominous grey and the wind was whipping the dried leaves into eddies around the wheels of her carriage. As she was helped up into it, the first large drops of rain fell. By the time they were back at her home, the rain was lashing against the sides of the coach and, in spite of the windows being closely drawn up, a cold wind was whistling around her. The Dowager pulled her shawl more tightly around herself and shivered, chilled to the bone.

The footman held an umbrella over her head as she dismounted, but the wild wind blew the rain under it, soaking her flimsy gown and shawl. She was soaked before she got in her front door. Her butler called for her dresser, hot water for a bath, and pressed a glass of brandy upon her. She was out of her wet things and bundled up by the fire in under an hour, and the whole household expressed its sincere hope that their mistress had not caught a chill. The lady herself pooh-poohed it, of course, refusing to admit that she should have listened to the advice about wearing warmer clothing at her age.

As she lay in bed that night, still feeling chilled, in spite of a warm brick at her feet and a roaring fire in her bedchamber, she considered what her friend had said. Was Cecilia Beaumaris intending to have her own establishment and girls' school after being married? She had assured the Dowager that her inheritance amounted only to a competence, but she had dismissed with what looked like real anger the idea that she wanted Tommy's money.

Where did Tommy fit in all this? He seemed to figure very little in the girl's plans. Why then had they become betrothed? Cecilia had answered that question strangely: because Tommy was kind, he made her laugh and they both disliked being importuned. Being importuned how? Suddenly the scales fell from Lady Broome's eyes. She had a pang of most unaccustomed guilt when she thought how often she had urged Tommy to marry this girl or that. He had laughed it off, as he did most things, but what if he was seriously vexed by it? And if people thought the Beaumaris girl had a fortune, she had probably received unwanted addresses. They must have made a pact to become engaged to put an end to all that. The more she thought about it, the more she convinced herself that this was the solution to the mystery. But was the betrothal real? That was the question.

The irony was that the Dowager had really taken to Cecilia. Although she had pushed a series of girls in his way, she had never really felt that any one of them was good enough for her Tommy. All of them had been well born and pretty enough but were otherwise unremarkable. She might chastise her grandson for his frippery ways, but she knew that, at heart, he was a good boy, with a fine sense of what was due to the family. After meeting Cecilia, she had been both relieved and encouraged. She would make Tommy an excellent wife. She was obviously of good family, though everyone knew her mother and father had been decidedly odd; she was well educated, had good manners and was sensible, but had an easy laugh. She was also strikingly good looking and dressed well, so that one need not be ashamed to call her Lady Broome. The Dowager was a woman of great determination. She was not going to let Miss Beaumaris slip through Tommy's fingers. She smiled to herself as she fell asleep, resolutely ignoring the tickle at the back of her throat.

Chapter Eleven

In spite of her somewhat disappointing interview with Mr. Davis, Cecilia wrote to Mr. Pounds to take him up on his offer of visiting him in Portsmouth, and began to plan how she could best travel there. When she enquired, she was told that the mail coach was the fastest mode of transportation, outside of private coaches. It would take about fifteen hours to get there, with three short stops to change the horses, when the passengers might dismount. But she could not count on getting so much as a cup of tea, since the ostlers worked with great speed. The mail coaches operated on a very strict timetable. Often, mail was simply thrown to and from the coaches as they passed through towns. It was also quite expensive. There were only four inside seats and a few more outside next to the driver and they had to be booked in advance. She was wondering if she could afford it, together with the cost of staying at an inn in Portsmouth at least one night, and perhaps two, without dipping into her bank balance. The reserves she had saved were fast disappearing. On the whole, though, she thought it would be money well spent, as she would learn more about the Ragged School in one visit than in a twelvemonth of letters. She had no experience of travelling far and on her own, and it never occurred to her that a well-dressed, good-looking woman travelling alone might be the object of speculation or even unwanted attention.

When Tommy called for her to visit the Vauxhall Gardens a few days later, she told him that this would be her last outing with him for a while.

"First of all, Tommy, I can't keep wearing the same gowns over and over, and I can't afford new ones. And before you say a word, no! I shall not allow you to buy any more for me. In less than six months I won't need them anymore, and I don't want to waste either my or your money for such a fleeting benefit. I've seen my man of business and he tells me that with what I have, it will be difficult enough to do what I want as it is." She held up her hand as Tommy started to speak. "Please don't embarrass me by offering me money. And don't give me the excuse you always use about your heart breaking. I'm convinced it must be made of sterner stuff!"

He turned to her. "Cecilia! My dear! You wrong me. I would never offer you money. I'm wounded you should think so. I can think of only one reason to offer a woman money and I can readily see that it would be embarrassing for both of us, but mostly for me, as you would be bound to refuse."

Cecilia blushed. "You know that's not what I mean! Be serious!"

"I'm always serious about such … transactions. Both parties need to know exactly what they are getting, to be sure of avoiding disappointment on one side or the other. And you are wrong about my heart. It is the most tender organ. It is already sick at the prospect of seeing poor girls in your establishment, deprived of a useful and happy future because you forbid me to help your school in any way. While I would not dream of offering *you* money, I consider it my duty as a gentleman and a Christian, to help with an institution of learning. What greater felicity could there be for someone of my seriousness of purpose?"

Since Tommy, in preparation for the Vauxhall Gardens, well known to be a place where extravagances of all sorts could pass without censure, was wearing a coat patterned after that of the

Harlequin, Cecilia could only laugh. The front left-hand side was red and the right-hand gold. In the back, the colors were reversed. The sleeves were checkered with both colors and the waistcoat was blue and white stripes. He looked like the Joker from a deck of cards, albeit a very handsome one.

"Oh Tommy! You are impossible!" laughed Cecilia. "But, you know, I want the school to be my own, and I don't want to be beholden to anyone. Please don't insist. Anyway, the second reason I shall not be seeing you for a while is that I am going to Portsmouth to visit Mr. Pounds' Ragged School. I can obtain a place on the Mail Coach next Wednesday – not before, can you believe, it's so booked up – and allowing for a day of travelling, two days of business and a day back, followed by, I'm sure, a needed period of recuperation, as I understand the roads do not make for a very comfortable ride, I shall not see you for perhaps ten days."

Tommy stared at her. "The Mail? Travelling to Portsmouth on the Mail? Never!" he replied, shock written large on his face. "That, at least, is something I can and shall do something about. As fiancée of the head of the august House of Broome, there is no question of your going anywhere on a Mail Coach. I forbid it. The honor of the family forbids it. My grandmother would certainly forbid it. She likes you; you know. Congratulated me on my good taste in snagging you in the face of aggressive opposition. Anyway, to return to the trip to Portsmouth. You will use my post chaise and I shall accompany you. Where are we going? Give me the direction so I may write to bespeak rooms in a suitable lodging place."

"But Tommy! Why on earth should you wish to go to Portsmouth? I believe it is a dirty, low place. You would dislike it intensely! Your coat would probably be ruined."

"If it is a dirty, low place, all the more reason for you not to go alone. And though my coat is, of course, of prime importance, it is not more important than you. No, Cecilia, I really cannot countenance it. It is your turn not to insist. Tell me when you wish to go and leave the rest to me."

Nothing Cecilia could say would shift her betrothed from this position, so at last she gave in. She was also touched that he should say he held her in higher esteem than his coat, not that she believed it. Nevertheless, it was fixed that he would call for her at ten in the morning the following Wednesday.

Now paying more attention to their journey to Vauxhall, Cecilia could see that they had left Mayfair and the gaslights of the city behind them. They crossed the Thames at the new Vauxhall Bridge, built just three years before. Then from a distance they could see the glow of Vauxhall Gardens against the evening sky. Cecilia was intrigued to see this place she had heard so much about, but never before visited.

There had been pleasure gardens on the site for over a hundred years, but in the middle of the previous century it had been expanded and embellished. The former Prince of Wales, uncle of the present king, had taken a particular interest in it and had his own pavilion built there. The fashion for the highly ornate rococo decoration was then at its height, and French and Italian artists had worked on the famous ceiling of the Rotunda, which looked rather like two very ornate fans opened against each other and forming a circle. The rich and fashionable would stroll down the arched entrance into the central hall where orchestras would play serious music, including that of Mr. Handel, whose statue had once stood under one of the triumphal arches in the South Walk.

In the last half-century, the grandeur of the Gardens had significantly diminished and these days the entertainments were less serious. Hot air balloons, tightrope walkers and concerts of popular music replaced Mozart and Handel, and the evening often ended with fireworks. Masquerades, when the participants would be masked and cloaked to cover their identity, encouraged licentious behavior from young people at all levels of society. This evening, Tommy had brought Cecilia to enjoy what was, in all probability, the last fine evening of the year, to eat the famous shaved ham and drink the infamous rack punch, which he warned her to be wary of. It tasted like barley water but was not called *punch* for nothing.

They would watch the world, fashionable, and not so fashionable, go by from the comfort of a private booth. These stood round the center of the Gardens. They were open on both sides, the better to enjoy the views, but in the evening, painted canvas backdrops depicting the glories of England were released down the back. At a stroke, thousands of gas lamps were illuminated throughout the gardens, hanging from poles and tree branches. The effect was magical. Cecilia gasped as they came through the gates. In this milieu, Tommy's harlequin coat looked perfectly appropriate. She was wearing her sapphire blue evening gown with the fur-lined cloak. In her hair she had only the pretty pin that held her ball plumes. She thought that if it were cool enough later to necessitate wearing the hood of her cloak, the plumes themselves would definitely be *de trop*. As a couple they looked stunning, and they attracted no little notice as they walked slowly down the center allée to the booth Tommy had bespoken.

Over the last few weeks, Cecilia had become accustomed to this wonderfully easy existence. Tommy had imperceptibly insinuated himself into her life. Without appearing in any way to impose, he organized sorties, took her driving in the park, picked her up for parties or the opera, arranged dinners, and when he found she was interested in history and the arts, took her to galleries and museums. At one point, she protested that being betrothed gave her far less time than she had had before, to the point where she could hardly find time for her lessons with the housemaids. This led to her explaining how a conversation with one of the scullery maids had inspired her to start a school for illiterate girls in the East End. Tommy had listened, making little comment, but afterwards he always asked how her students were progressing, and often turned up with paper, pen, ink, pencils and even books that he said he had discovered in the nursery at Broome House.

Amongst these was an illustrated Aesop's Fables. It proved a very good teaching tool. The stories were short, the illustrations conveyed the idea of the text and the moral of the tale always made for interesting discussions.

"A wolf in sheep's clothin'," said Bridget, when they read that fable. "Just like the butcher's boy. Ever so nice 'e seems, all smilin' an' sweet. Then the other day 'e gets me be'ind the back door and tries to kiss me!"

"Go on! 'E never did!' said Rose, "'E did the same to me last week!"

"That rotten bugger!" exclaimed Bridget. "Well, next time I sees 'im I'm tellin' 'im, 'you're a wolf in sheep's clothin', that's what you are Mickey me-lad, so stick to yer liver 'n kidneys 'n don't come sniffin' roun' me no more!'"

Cecilia couldn't help laughing. "I applaud the sentiment, but perhaps not the way it's couched," she said, knowing the girls would look puzzled. "What I mean is, what you say is right but the way you say it could be better. There are ways of talking, I'm sure you know. And how you speak determines what people think of you. If you want to be an upstairs maid you have to learn to speak like one. Listen to Mr. Bromley or Mrs. Browning and try to imitate them."

"Don't say *bugger* no more?" suggested Rose.

"Exactly," said Cecilia.

She reported this exchange to Tommy in its entirety, since she knew he would not be shocked by her using a minor vulgarity, and anyway, she had a knack for imitating accents. He laughed uproariously and said his Fable book had never been used by a more appreciative audience. But he took her point about needing more time for her lessons, and from then on made arrangements either for the afternoon or the evening, but not both. Nonetheless, she found herself more looked after and catered to than ever before in her life, and often had to tell herself sternly that this was only for the next few months, and not to become too accustomed to it.

Her plans for setting up a school had met with a distinct check, in that the amount of money available to her was proving insufficient for even her minimum needs. Mr. Davis had been as good as his word, and had investigated the availability of properties for rent that would be suitable both for her dwelling and for a school. He wrote to her at least once a week, saying he had been to see possible locations, but had so far been thwarted.

> *The problem is, my dear Miss Beaumaris,* he wrote, *one is able to find houses to rent in suitable areas, but if the cost is affordable, the place is too*

small, comprising usually only one room downstairs, with a scullery, and two more upstairs. I cannot think that your teachers would be happy with only one room for all the activities of daily life as well as holding classes, and the upstairs would, of course, be needed as bedchambers. Larger establishments are available, but these are in less salubrious environs and are attended by the evils of dirt and rats and, sad to say, often drunken neighbors. The regard our firm holds for your late parents and yourself does not permit us to recommend such a milieu.

Cecilia shuddered at the idea of living with rats and was very discouraged by these reports. But she determined to put it all out of her mind for the time being, as she looked forward to her trip to Portsmouth.

She had made a point of informing herself about that city. She discovered that, while it was not itself mentioned in the Domesday Book, settlements that later became the town of Portsmouth are mentioned. It had for centuries been the chief naval base of England, being possessed of a natural and sheltered deep-water harbor, and its history was one of almost constant attack from the French. On one infamous occasion in 1338, this long-time enemy sailed ships into Portsmouth harbor flying English flags and then proceeded to rape and pillage the town. However, redress could be said to have been obtained, albeit nearly five centuries later, by the great victory at Trafalgar the whole nation had been inflamed by, a little over ten years before.

In 1805, Admiral Lord Nelson left Portsmouth with a fleet of thirty-three led by his great ship *Victory* to engage the combined French and Spanish fleet of forty-one in the Battle of Trafalgar.

Although greatly outnumbered in ships and men, Nelson defeated the enemy, which lost twenty-two ships while the British lost none. The great cost to the nation was the loss of Nelson himself, shot by a French musketeer just before the end of the battle. Although not of a warlike or vengeful disposition, Cecilia's heart rose as she read and remembered how Nelson had defied traditional naval warfare tactics and, instead of facing the enemy in a parallel line, sailed two rows of ships directly into the center. Confused and routed, the enemy allowed twenty-one ships to be captured and over fifteen thousand men to be lost or wounded, compared with under two thousand on the British side.

On the following Wednesday promptly at ten in the morning, two coaches emblazoned with the Broome Coat of Arms arrived at Bruton Street. One contained his lordship's valet and a not insignificant volume of luggage, and from the other leaped a very smartly dressed Tommy, ready to accompany Cecilia to Portsmouth. He was wearing a long black wool greatcoat over pale lemon britches and top boots. Only glimpses of his jacket could be seen, but it appeared, for Tommy, to be very sober indeed, of navy superfine. But this was compensated for by the glory of his waistcoat which, when revealed, was shown to be of navy silk embroidered all over with a gold design that proved to be large bumble bees. Over one of her day dresses, Cecilia wore her pelisse and the bonnet Tommy had given her. In a bag, other than nightclothes and necessaries, she had packed only the altered wool skirt and waistcoat she had worn at Highmount, thinking that would be most appropriate for visiting a Ragged School. She had not considered the need for more than the one gown she had on, and she had packed no evening clothes at all. But as a groom picked up her bag and looked questioningly around for more, she began to have doubts. The bag was placed in the second coach where Brooke, the valet, regarded it askance and asked if that was all there was. When told it was, his eyebrows nearly disappeared under his neat bowler hat. He remembered occasions when he had travelled with his master and his current inamorata and there had scarcely been room for himself amongst the piles of trunks and bandboxes. And this was his lordship's betrothed!

The groom was lowering the steps for Cecilia when Tommy looked around and said, "Where's your abigail?"

"Abigail?" she answered in surprise. "I don't have one."

Looking shocked, Tommy took her elbow and led her aside. "My dear, you must know you cannot travel alone for a long distance in a covered carriage, and much less stay overnight in any inn with a single gentleman and no maid or chaperone!"

"But ... but ..." stuttered Cecilia, "I didn't think!"

"Well, we must think now. Is there someone who can accompany you?"

Cecilia looked at him for a moment and then ran downstairs. She found the housekeeper, and explained the situation, asking if Bridget could be spared for a few days. Mrs. Browning, though by tradition called Mrs., had never been married. However, in her thin, bird-like frame she nurtured a romantic disposition that had been put into a flutter by the betrothal of Cecilia, whom she had come to admire. So she at once agreed that Bridget could be spared, only asking whether Miss Beaumaris might prefer to take one of the upstairs maids, who were perhaps more presentable. But Cecilia saw this as an opportunity to further Bridget's education – they were, after all, going to visit a school – and begged leave to take her young protégée. Bridget herself could not believe her luck. She flew up to her room, threw off her apron, tossed a few items into a shawl and knotted it into a bundle. She pulled her ragged cloak around her shoulders and was ready to leave in under ten minutes.

When she came out of the house with her bundle, Tommy looked at her with misgiving, but directed her to the coach with his valet, whose eyebrows disappeared under his hat as if never to return. Before climbing in next to Cecilia, Tommy had a quick word with the coachman.

"We are going to make a quick stop at my Grandmother's," he announced as he sat down.

Cecilia was a little surprised, but said nothing. When they arrived at the Dowager Lady Broome's townhouse, Tommy led both women into the hall, Bridget still clutching her bundle, under the haughty gaze of her ladyship's very superior butler, whose name, Cecilia remembered, was Mobley. Tommy had a few quiet words with him then turned back to them.

"Bridget will need a more … suitable wardrobe," he said, smiling kindly at the maid. My grandmother's housekeeper will take care of it."

A plump, cheerful woman who Tommy greeted as Robbie came into the hall, bobbed a curtsey, took one look at Bridget and pushed her by the shoulders towards the nether regions of the house, saying, "Have no fear, my lord. We can sort this out in a shake."

"My grandmother has always had such a large complement of housemaids that there is certainly something to fit Bridget somewhere," said Tommy, leading her into the drawing room. "Sit here for a minute while Mobley sends to see if granny is fit to receive us. But don't be surprised if the answer is no. She isn't usually seen downstairs before noon." And he ushered Cecilia into the charmingly feminine room with the pink shaded windows.

Cecilia hardly knew what to say. Once again, she found herself overwhelmed by Tommy's cavalier assurance. Looking at it dispassionately, it was obvious that Bridget's scullery-maid uniform was hardly suitable for the abigail of Lord Broome's betrothed. Still, she felt he should have at least asked her! She was on the point of remonstrating with him when she thought, if he had asked her, what could she have said? So instead, she just smiled at him.

"Thank you, Tommy! You have a knack of solving my problems before I even realize I have them. But your grandmother will wonder at our sudden appearance, surely?"

Before Tommy could answer, the butler returned and said, "Her ladyship sends her regrets but she prefers not to receive anyone at the moment."

"There, what did I tell you?" exclaimed Tommy. "She won't see anyone before spending at least two hours with her dresser. And she criticizes me for the time I spend with Brooke!"

The old butler was on the verge of telling him the truth. In fact, the Dowager had not been well since her soaking on the day she visited Lady March. She was suffering from a racking cough and had not left her bed for two days. She steadfastly refused to send for the doctor, saying that she would be right as rain if people would just stop fussing. When she heard her grandson and his betrothed were in the house, she took one look at herself in her hand mirror and denied all possibility of an audience.

"But tell him to come back in two days and bring Cecilia with him," she said gasping a little, "I want to talk to them both."

Receiving this command, Tommy in turn sent a message that in two days they would probably still be in Portsmouth, but they would come back as soon as they could.

In about half an hour, Bridget was back, looking as fine as fivepence in a simple black wool dress with detachable white collar and cuffs. She had also been given a cloak, which, though it was old, was in far better condition than her own, and sported a somewhat faded gold braid around the hood, ending in tassels for tying at the neck. She was ecstatic.

"Look, Miss," she said, twirling around, "they give me this dress that's too small for all the maids what's working here now, and Mrs. Robinson found me two sets of collars and cuffs. I got a bag 'n all, to put me stuff in!" She held up a leather bag, which, like the cloak, was somewhat battered, but was infinitely better than the old shawl bundle.

"Then we'd better be off if we want to make Guildford today," said Tommy, and led his two ladies, one who looked like a queen, and the other holding her head as high as one, out of the house.

Brooke was somewhat mollified by the improved appearance of his travelling companion but was still inclined to be haughty, until she won him round by her artless comments on what they passed by. Never having been out of London in her life, Bridget was enchanted and amazed by the sights. Since Brooke had been with the Earl since he left Oxford, he had travelled widely in Britain and on the Continent and adopted a blasé attitude towards the glories of Surrey. Bridget found him wondrously superior, and her reverent attention to his every word soon gave him quite a good opinion of her, and an even better one of himself.

Cecilia was also regaling her companion, who however, was looking at her with amusement rather than reverence. She had brought with her the book on the history of Portsmouth, and lost no time in informing Tommy what she had discovered.

"'Pon my soul, Cecilia!" he exclaimed. "It's like travellin' with my old tutor! When I did the Grand Tour after Eton, he used to sit just like you, prosin' on about the Lord knows what. All I wanted to do was look at the pretty girls and … er … *talk* to a couple of them, you know, but he kept on about columns and statues and vistas. The only vista I was interested in was that of a comely pair of ankles. We were pretty hemmed in at Eton! Took quite a bit to shake him off, I can tell you! Luckily, my …erm … nether regions got a bit chafed by sitting in the coach too long and I was able to tell him I thought I had scarlet fever. Managed to persuade the sawbones to tell him a Banbury Tale, too. Offered him a monkey to say I had to stay in bed for a few days quietly in the dark. Soon as I could, I bundled my bedclothes up to look as if I was sleeping and took myself off. Saw a good few vistas, I can tell you!"

Cecilia could not help laughing at this, but shook her head, imagining the handsome young heir to an earldom let loose amongst the fleshpots of Europe. "But didn't he realize the subterfuge?"

"Only after I'd been gone twenty-four hours. When I got back he was sitting in my room looking like Death eating a cracker. He offered to flog me, but I looked him in the eye and dared him to try. He could see my experiences had made a man of me, and after that he let me alone in the evenings. I still had to look at all the statues with their heads and arms and ... well ... you know what, broken off. I still think it was a hum! We went all that way to see a lot of coves that were only half there. And why were they all naked? I know it's pretty hot in some of those places in the summer, but in the winter? Probably that's why they took to wearing togas. Just grabbed the first thing they could find – a tablecloth, probably – and wrapped it round." He seemed lost in memory for a moment, then concluded, "Still, it was interestin', I suppose, especially the vistas." He grinned engagingly at her.

It really was very difficult to be serious with Tommy, Cecilia realized. She gave it one last try. "It's so sad that Admiral Lord Nelson died at Trafalgar. It was his greatest moment. I suppose he knew he'd made history, though."

"Made history? I should say so! For a man with only one eye and one arm he had a way with the ladies that's the stuff of legends. Women used to fall into his arms, or arm, I should say. I remember being at a party one time when I was about twenty and thought myself a hell of a fellow. I was doing pretty well with one young thing, or so I thought, when all of a sudden, I was talking to the pillar she'd been leanin' against. The Great Admiral had just arrived, and she'd run off to see him, along with all the other women in the place. Never knew what they saw in him; his coat was nothing to write home about and his neckcloth was a rag. There was the patch, of course. Made him look dashed exciting. Thought of wearing one myself, but m'mother asked me if I was forming a sty and offered to put some salve on it, so I gave it up."

The seriousness with which he announced all this was belied by the twinkle in his eye, and, again, Cecilia could not help laughing. "Oh Tommy! Don't you take anything seriously?"

"You're serious enough for both of us, m'dear," he answered. "I haven't known you very long, but I get the impression that nothing much has made you laugh in your life up till now."

Reflecting on this, Cecilia thought it was true. She had never been really unhappy, but never exactly joyous, either. As a young girl who had never known deep affection, the loving kindness of Laura Warren had been her salvation, and her friendship as she grew older had been the rock she depended on. But both she and Laura had been of a naturally serious disposition, and she could remember very few occasions for laughter or silliness. So, hesitantly at first, she began to tell Tommy about her life: her scientist parents who, lost in their own ideas, often forgot she existed, the series of nannies who had all been quite kind but frankly puzzled by the long-legged little girl with the serious gaze, and then her time at school, first as a pupil, then as a teacher.

"It's true," she said at last. "I haven't really been in the way of laughing at things. But, for all that, I don't want you to think I've been unhappy or at all to be pitied."

If he thought that what she described sounded very sad indeed, Tommy made no answer to this, but simply smiled and changed the subject.

Chapter Twelve

They drove to The Angel Inn in Guildford, where they would spend the night. Tommy explained to Cecilia that for propriety's sake he had told them to make up a truckle bed in her room for her maid, assuming all along that she had one. The Angel was an ancient coaching inn dating, they said, from the 1300's. The black oak beams and low ceilings certainly gave the impression of antiquity, and, as they climbed the stairs to bed after a less than mediocre dinner, which Tommy complained had probably been cooked in the 1300's and kept warm for half a century, he commented there were probably mice in the walls.

"If you should be afraid in the night, just call my name," he said as he took her to her door. "I'm a fearless mouse slayer. All my friends will tell you."

"Just like Dick Whittington's cat, then," replied Cecilia, and then had to explain about Bridget's reading material.

"Perhaps I shall hear the Bells calling to me to be Lord Mayor of London when I return," he said, as he left her. "I should like wearing that enormous chain, but sable don't become me. I'd have to have the cloak made over in ermine or chinchilla."

Cecilia was laughing and shaking her head as she went in to bed.

The next morning, bright and early, they started for Petersfield, where they would change horses before the final descent into Portsmouth. This town, which lay at the northern edge of the South Downs, was on a much-travelled route both east-west and north-south. Luckily, they arrived the day after the weekly fair which featured trading in cattle of all sorts, and generally resulted in considerable congestion in the center. As the ostlers changed the horses at the Red Lion Inn, the innkeeper's wife invited Cecilia to take a look at the Physick Garden, but it was already the middle of the afternoon and they had still nearly twenty miles to go, so regretfully, after a quick cup of tea, they moved off.

Their ride took them over the South Downs, and in a few places, Tommy asked if, to save the horses on a steep uphill climb, she would mind if they walked. Glad to be outside and stretching her legs in the crisp clean air, Cecilia strode pace for pace with his lordship, a fact which she did not notice, but which gave him a good deal of pleasure, accustomed as he was to adjusting his long stride to that of damsels who complained he walked too fast.

As they came over Portsdown Hill into Portsmouth, a glorious view met their eyes. To the right the autumn sun was sinking into the sea in a last glory of red and gold, the purple night sky above. In the distance just off the coast, lay the Isle of Wight, gold-tipped. Towards them, in the arms of Portsmouth harbor, stood the habitations of the town, the rooftops just tinted red with the last of the sun. Closer below, following the now almost black thicketed slope of the Downs they could see the crenellations of Portchester Castle, dating from the time of the Romans, outlined against the darkening sky. Unbidden, the driver reined in the horses, as the sun sank below the horizon, leaving a few trails of its outstretched fingers against the sky.

"This is where Mr. Pounds brings his pupils when he can," whispered Cecilia, struck almost wordless by the scene. "How beautiful it is!"

It was fully dark by the time they reached the George Inn in Portsmouth where Tommy had reserved rooms. This was another very old, dark-beamed place but very far from the glories of the view from the top of the hill. Raucous singing rang from the taproom, interspersed with oaths and scuffles. Mine host apologized, but said that the sailors were a rowdy crowd and needed only a glass or two before they started in with their shanties, their hornpipes, and, inevitably, their fisticuffs.

Bridget was thrilled by it all and wanted to peek into the taproom to see some real sailors, until forcibly prevented by Brooke, who sniffed haughtily at such low company and entertainment. Tommy just laughed and told the host to put forth his best effort for dinner, as they had been almost poisoned at the Angel in Guildford. The innkeeper said it did not surprise him; he had heard they kept a very poor table. His rib, he declared, had prepared a tender side of lamb reared on the Downs and kicking up its heels only yesterday, a fish pie made from a couple of plaice so fresh they thought they were still in the Solent, and as lovely a parsnip pudding as you ever ate. There was also a piece of beef, should his lordship require it. Tommy gave hearty assent to the whole menu and said they would be ready in half an hour to eat it.

"Half an hour, my lord?" exclaimed Brooke as they were mounting the stairs. "It's not possible! It will take more than that to change your coat!"

"I'm not changing it," replied his lordship, calmly.

Brooke's face assumed the color of an overripe tomato. "Not change your coat, my lord?" he stuttered. "But you've worn it all day!"

Closing the bedroom door behind him, Tommy eyed his valet severely. "It cannot have escaped your notice that Miss Beaumaris has been wearing the same gown for two days. You will, moreover, have noticed that she brought very little with her. I shall therefore not change for dinner. Indeed, I regret having done so yesterday."

"But my lord, I packed enough for two changes every day, not including evening wear!" cried his man, much overwrought. "I've never known you not to change for dinner! I have my reputation to consider!"

"Your reputation be damned," replied Tommy, calmly. "If mine can stand it, so can yours. And if you are able to find a person in this place who knows a good piece of tailoring from a tablecloth, I'll give you ten guineas. Now fetch some hot water, and make sure Miss Beaumaris has some. I doubt that maid of hers has thought of it."

Brooke left the room, muttering imprecations about unreasonable employers who did not know when they were well off and since when was it his job to be a lady's maid? His mood was not improved by finding Bridget in the kitchen, who far from not thinking about hot water, had already taken some up to her mistress and was in a fair way to becoming bosom bows with the landlady. But when the newly minted abigail introduced him as the *ever so clever an' nice Mr. Brooke what 'as been with 'is lordship for fifteen year and knows everythin'*, he allowed himself to be mollified, especially as it was flavored by the delicious cooking smells and the invitation to sit 'imself at the 'ead of the table as soon as 'e could get away, an' they was right proud to 'ave 'im in their kitchen. He returned to his master with the ewer of hot water and commented that the staff of the George seemed to be very good people, if simple in their ways.

The betrothed couple dined together in great good humor. Cecilia noticed Tommy had not changed, which reassured her very much. The night before when he had appeared for dinner resplendent in full evening dress, she had regretted not bringing a change of clothing for the evening. It had never even occurred to her.

Her crumpled gown was even worse today and she had almost sent word that she would eat in her room, but the thought of abandoning Tommy to an evening of shanties and hornpipes made her change her mind. How much she had to learn about the ways of the *ton*, she thought, and then tried to console herself that in a few months she could forget all about it. But somehow, that promise seemed less golden than it had before. She realized that she really enjoyed being with Tommy, and the thought that he would quite soon disappear from her orbit gave her an odd feeling in her heart.

They were due to meet John Pounds the following afternoon. In spite of their being very road-weary, sleep had been slow in coming because of the unbridled celebrations from the taproom below, so the whole group slept late the next morning. It was not until after luncheon that they made their way to the Ragged School on St. Mary's Street. Cecilia had asked that Bridget go with them, but Brooke stayed behind. Unbending from his usual *hauteur*, he suggested that Bridget bring him Miss Beaumaris's much abused gown, so that he could try to furbish it up for that evening. He was sure he said, eying with disapproval her made-over skirt and waistcoat, that Miss Beaumaris would be desirous of changing for dinner. His chief objective was, of course, to persuade his lordship to do likewise, since his pride could not bear the sight of his master again going down for dinner in his day clothes.

In the meantime, the coachman had ascertained the location of Mr. Pounds' establishment. "Bound to be a nasty, low place," he announced as they mounted into the carriage. 'Ole town is. Why, it's running over with vermin and the 'ouses is so small and 'ung over the streets yer can 'ardly drive down some o' them. And the stink!"

They left the George Inn on Queen Street and drove down past the dockyard towards their destination. It was true that the town of Portsmouth, in common with ports the world over, was not a beautiful place and a pervading odor of rotten fish and decay hung in the air. The wealthier citizens built their mansions out towards the North End of the town, but down by the docks it was bustling and obviously prosperous enough, crowded with dray carts piled high with barrels and bales moving ponderously through the streets. Sailors were everywhere, particularly around the doorways to the public houses that appeared to be on every corner. Shouts of laughter and anger and snatches of song came from most of them, even though it was only just after two in the afternoon.

As they passed the wide main gate of the dockyard, beyond the smoke arising from innumerable chimneys, they could see the masts of some of the great vessels that made up the 684 ship fleet of the Royal Navy.

"Apparently they are now using steam to power the pumps and woodworking machinery," said Tommy, who had quietly done a little investigation of his own before coming to the town. "And they have ironworks and copper smelting right in the dockyard. Except for the ships, it could be a scene from the Inferno!"

"I didn't know you had read Dante," said Cecilia. "Did you read it in Italian?"

"Good lord, no," responded her betrothed in some amusement. "In English. One of the beaks at Eton gave us a taste of Dante one term. It made a change from Latin and Greek. We were all looking forward to the second circle of hell, where the lustful are condemned, you remember, thinking it would be full of salacious description. But alas, no! They are just buffeted about by a fearful wind. That's about it. Bit of a bore, really. We were all disappointed, after reading all that for nothing!"

"But the hope of excitement made you read it!" laughed Cecilia, "I must remember that as an inducement for my pupils."

They had by now arrived at John Pounds' place of business, an ordinary enough cobbler's shop in an ugly, flat fronted row of shops and houses on one of the dark, narrow streets the coachman had complained about. The sight of his lordship's carriage on St. Mary's Street caused no little stir. The carriage effectively blocked the whole street, so his lordship sent it away, saying they would take a hackney back to The George. Then he and his betrothed and her abigail went into the shop.

They were met by a comforting smell mixed of leather and cooking. The cobbler, moving sometimes with a crutch and sometimes without, seemed perfectly at ease with his affluent visitors, and invited them to sit, or look around, as they pleased. He continued with his work, deftly re-soling boots on a metal last which could be turned to take different shoe sizes. He placed a piece of leather on the heel or sole of the boot, quickly tapped small nails around the perimeter and then cut the excess leather away. He wore a leather apron with a large front pocket from which he withdrew the tools he needed. Cecilia found it almost mesmerizing to watch him as he worked quickly and surely, without a wasted motion.

The room was about twenty feet long and twelve feet wide, with a door in the back that stood open into what must have been a scullery and from which the smells of cooking were emanating. All along both sides of the room were shelves at about shoulder height, filled with tattered books, newspapers and magazines. Some writing slates lay higgledy-piggledy here and there. Below the shelves was a row of benches on each side. It looked as if the benches might hold ten children each, but Mr. Pound had told her he sometimes had as many as forty.

"It must be very crowded in here," she remarked.

"Yes, it often is, but I never turn anyone away. The children sit on the floor, or the smaller ones on the bigger ones' laps. Somehow, we manage. They aren't used to having their own place, you see, Madam. At home it's the same. There can be six or eight children in a family with a Ma and Pa, and likely as not, a Granny or Grandad. They all live in a room no bigger than this and they're lucky to have a bed between them. So no one thinks it's too crowded!"

Bridget was looking at the materials on the shelves: the books, newspapers and slates, finally sitting down to look at one of the books. Tommy wandered around, even looking into the scullery. He had removed his greatcoat, for it was quite warm, and, as the little room grew darker, he glowed like some sort of bird of paradise. He had chosen to wear the Harlequin coat from the night at Vauxhall and Bridget had not been able to take her eyes off him earlier. Though it had shocked Cecilia when he appeared in it at luncheon, when the children began to arrive, she saw why he had chosen it. They were dazzled and drawn to him in equal measure. They certainly were not afraid of him.

"Allo Gov'nor," said one boy, a little bolder than the rest, who by his size looked about seven years old but who could easily have been twelve, "wot'yer doin' 'ere in that coat? You goin' to a party?"

"No, my man," replied Tommy seriously. "I'm wearing it in your honor. I thought you might like it. Do you?"

"Not 'alf!" exclaimed the boy. "Where d'yer get it?"

"My tailor in London made it. I'm gratified it meets with your approval." Then, as the urchin looked puzzled, "I'm glad you like it. Tell you what. You do everything Mr. Pounds here asks you to do. Learn to read and write, then write me a letter telling me so and I'll buy you a coat like this. Here's my card." He gave the urchin the elegant piece of vellum which read:

Allenby, Broome House, Grosvenor Square, London

The urchin looked at the card as if it were handed down from Mount Sinai, and stuffed it in his pocket. At that, all the other boys clamored for a card, which Tommy willingly gave them, on the same condition.

Then one of the girls, who had been holding back, said shyly, "If you please, Sir. I don't need a coat like yourn – though it's ever so nice."

"Of course you don't, Madam," replied his lordship, with a bow. "You shall have a new gown. But you must write and tell me you have finished your studies with Mr. Pounds."

Thereupon, all the girls claimed a new gown, and received a card from their Harlequin benefactor.

"Never had so many girls want to take m'card in m'life," remarked Tommy quietly but with some satisfaction. He sat down next to Cecilia on one of the few chairs in the room to prepare for what was obviously going to be the lesson of the day.

"But what will you do if they all write to you?" she whispered.

"Send them dresses, of course, though lord knows how I'll know what will suit each of them. I'll have to write back and ask the color of their eyes and hair."

"It will be bad enough for a gentleman to be sending young ladies dresses, without asking questions of a personal nature," remarked Cecilia.

"Do you think so?" replied her betrothed with an innocent air. "But my motives are always of the purest, as anyone who knows me can attest to."

She looked at him with the beginning of a frown, but saw the twinkle in his eye and chuckled.

"That's true. I let you buy me dresses after all," she said. "I never for a moment mistrusted your motives."

"Dear me," said Tommy softly. "That's a pity," and raised an eyebrow.

Cecilia blushed.

It was a good thing that they were all soon called to attention by Mr. Pounds and settled down to listen to him read an episode from a popular children's book entitled the *Life and*

Perambulations of a Mouse, in which a mouse called Nimble describes his life and observes the humans he encounters on his journeys. He overhears children being urged to be brave, kind and good natured, and, above all, to listen to their parents. However, he and his brothers forget the chief advice their own mother gave them, which was never to eat in the same place more than once, and two of them end up being killed. The description of the killing of the poor mice made Cecilia blink, but the children seemed to take it in their stride. She commented on it to Tommy.

"Yes, bloodthirsty little beggars, children," he answered. "I know I was. I had that book when I was little, and I liked the bits about killing the best."

"I wasn't allowed to read books like that, where animals act like people," said Cecilia. My parents disapproved of anything that wasn't real, or based on science. But I know now that children learn much quicker from stories like these than from all the science in the world. I shall certainly have that sort of reading material in my school."

After the reading, there was a discussion about what lessons might be learned from it, and then the class broke up into three groups. One group read from the books and papers on the shelves. The more experienced readers helped those who knew less. Another took the slates and practiced their letters, again led by more experienced pupils. The third group also used the slates to do elementary arithmetic, helped by small squares of wood that the youngsters could manipulate. Mr. Pounds himself called up his leaders one by one and moved them along in their own studies. In this way, everyone was able to make progress.

Bridget threw herself into both teaching and learning and proved herself so useful that Cecilia decided to ask her to come to live and work with her when the time came. Tommy moved amongst the young people, listening, occasionally correcting and always making them laugh. Cecilia was astonished to see that he made no objection when grubby hands clutched at his coat, or when chalk from the slates marked his perfect pantaloons. He seemed a different person.

Time flew by. Then Mr. Pounds clapped his hands and the pupils put away their books and slates. They disappeared into the scullery in groups, the youngest first, where they could be heard washing their hands before reappearing and sitting on the benches with a lump of bread and a wooden bowl of the stew that had been perfuming the air all afternoon. It was all done without jostling for place or jealousy, the older helping the younger before serving themselves. When Cecilia commented on this, the cobbler nodded and smiled.

"That is what I hope to achieve by reading them an improving tale and discussing morality before getting down to the lessons," he said. "Education is more than just reading, writing and arithmetic. They have to learn to live in the word: to give and take. Many of them have had to fight to stay alive and it's hard for them. But after a while they understand. As for the meal, it isn't much, mostly vegetables with a neck of mutton or the like, but they get it after one set of lessons. We change over after supper, the groups all switch round, then round again. That way, the ones who come only for the food are forced, you might say, into learning something before they can eat. A few leave after the meal, but most of them stay."

The visitors took the supper break as their signal to depart. The youngsters were sorry to see them go, especially Tommy, who they all flocked around, reminding him of his promises of coats and dresses. His lordship tried to press a roll of banknotes onto Mr. Pounds, but he resolutely refused, saying he had enough for his wants, and he had seen how money was the greatest source of corruption in society. Tommy put the money back in his billfold but the cobbler was gratified to receive, a couple of weeks later, a whole new set of books, slates and writing materials with the following note:

> *Aristotle said educating the mind without educating the heart is no education at all. Thank you for reminding me of Nimble the Mouse, who taught my heart as well as my mind.*
>
> Thomas Allenby, Earl of Broome

The second evening at The George passed much the same as the first, except that Cecilia was able to replace her skirt and waistcoat with her silk gown, which had indeed been much improved by the valet's ministrations. Tommy sat opposite her at dinner, not in full evening dress, which, to his almost tearful chagrin, was once again denied to Brooke, but in a long-tailed coat of blue superfine, with flawless pantaloons and boots that would have done very well for a mirror. With his golden wavy hair and elegant figure, he set all the maids hearts a-flutter. Even Cecilia, absorbed in thinking over what she had observed at the Ragged School that afternoon, was again struck by how very handsome he was.

The following morning, they began the return trip to London, this time staying overnight in Guildford and arriving back home in the mid-afternoon five days after they had left. Having deposited Cecilia in Bruton Street, Tommy was driven back to Grosvenor Square, where he was immediately accosted by his butler with the unwelcome news that his grandmother was seriously ill. Mobley had been sending for him.

Chapter Thirteen

After Tommy had left with Cecilia the Wednesday before, the Dowager Countess's cold and sore throat had continued to worsen. For two days, she had continued to refuse to see a doctor, but asked for a note to be sent round to Tommy. When the word came back that he was still from home, she fell back on her pillows with the first sign of weakness she had exhibited. The next day, when she was found to be unable even to sit up, her butler sent another note around to Tommy and then took it upon himself to call for the family physician. When this gentleman had examined her, he left the room shaking his head, saying her lungs were now so filled with fluid and her condition so weak that nothing could be done except to try to keep her comfortable and to trust in Providence.

Weak she might be, but the Dowager put her household in a flurry by refusing to lie still. She continually raised her head from her pillow demanding in querulous tones to see her man of business. In vain did her dresser, her maid and finally, Mobley, beg her to await Tommy's return.

"Be … too … late," she gasped. "Now … get him … now, I tell you!"

Her white face and the limp way she fell back onto her pillows frightened her servants so much that in the end they did as she asked and sent for her lawyer. When he arrived he was closeted with her for almost an hour, and came out as the doctor had done, shaking his head and looking very solemn indeed. Mobley sent yet another note to Tommy.

Receiving this last note as he stepped through the doors of Broome House after returning from Portsmouth, his lordship wasted no time. He immediately turned around, and in spite of his grandmother's vociferous dislike of male visitors daring to visit her improperly attired, did not even change his top boots before calling his carriage back. Not fifteen minutes later, he was in his grandmother's house. Only those who knew him well would have perceived from his appearance that he was in a fever of apprehension. His normally carefully disordered locks were frankly disheveled, his caped greatcoat was unbuttoned, and he was missing a kid glove. Completely oblivious to all this, he leaped up the stairs and it was only the dresser's hand on his arm and admonishing finger to her lips that stopped him from thrusting open the bedchamber door and striding in. He then realized his heart was beating uncomfortably fast and he made himself stop and take a deep breath before quietly turning the knob.

The sight of his grandmother so small, white and still in her great rose silk-draped bed made him catch his breath. Assuming a tone he was far from feeling, he went over to her bedside saying lightly,

"Come on, Gran! Stop shamming! I was only away for a few days, no need to go into a decline!"

He knelt by her bedside, took her small, cold hand in his, and kissed it, then held it to his cheek. Her eyes fluttered open and she turned her head on her pillow.

"S...silly boy!" she gasped. "It...It's all over with me. But want...wanted to see you."

"Don't say that, Granny," he faltered, tears coming to his eyes. "I'm here now. You'll come about. I need you. Who'll nag me if you don't?"

"N...never needed me, or ... anyone," she gasped again and, with what was obviously superhuman effort, she lifted her head and looked at him. "Marry her, Tommy!" Her head fell back and her voice was a whisper he had to strain to hear. "P...promise me you'll marry her."

"I will, grandmother," he replied in a low voice. "I will, if she'll have me. I promise." He bent his golden head over her hand and his tears fell freely now.

"Made her," sighed his grandmother, which Tommy misheard as *make her*, as the last rattle sounded in her throat.

He looked up at her dear old face, from which all the lines had begun to be magically erased, then bent his head and sobbed as if his heart would break. At length, his shoulders stopped heaving. He dried his eyes on a snow-white monogrammed handkerchief exactly like the one he had given Cecilia, took a deep breath, stood slowly up, kissed his grandmother on the hand, then on the cheek and went to the door.

"She's gone," he said briefly to the dresser and the butler who stood outside. Not trusting himself to say more, he muttered, "You know what to do." He went swiftly downstairs and outside. "I'll walk," he said to his coachman and strode down the street, his suspiciously bright eyes fixed on an unseen object.

"He'll take it bad," remarked Mobley, on whom his lordship's red eyes had not been lost. "Devoted to her, he was."

"Yes, in spite of her ringing a peal over him regularly ever since he was a boy" agreed the dresser. "Two peas in a pod they were."

On this the two old retainers separated, she into the Dowager's room and he downstairs to send a note to the firm of undertakers who had served the family for the last hundred years.

Tommy at last arrived at Grosvenor Square sufficiently recovered to be able to tell Brooke to find him a black coat and, since he was almost sure of possessing no black waistcoat, the most sober of those he had. He gave orders for black armbands for himself and the rest of the household and wrote to his tailor with orders for complete sets of mourning attire. He then spent the rest of the late afternoon and evening writing personal notes to family and those he knew to be close friends of his grandmother, to inform them of the sad news. His last note was to Cecilia. He left to his secretary the task of contacting the newspapers, as well as that of writing notes excusing him from all social engagements for the foreseeable future.

He had finished making a very poor dinner, though the cook had prepared everything she could that might tempt him, and was sitting in the drawing room staring unseeingly into the fire when there was a ring at the door bell. He was astonished to see Cecilia being ushered in and automatically rose to his feet.

In his black coat, dark waistcoat and pantaloons, he looked quite unlike himself, and she ran towards him, her arms outstretched saying, "Oh, my poor Tommy! I'm so sorry! I just had to come!"

The butler withdrew quickly, but not before seeing her take both Tommy's hands in her own and bring them to her heart.

"Quite right, too," said that stately gentleman to the housekeeper. "There's those might say a young woman shouldn't visit a single man in his home in the evening, especially arriving in a hack, as she did, but I say, if she can cheer him up after such a terrible shock, why not?"

In fact, Tommy did exclaim at the impropriety of Cecilia coming to his home alone, late at night and in a hackney, though the sight of her did bring him comfort.

"Oh, Tommy, who cares for propriety at a moment like this?" she said softly in her low, musical voice, looking at his drawn features and bloodshot eyes, "I only knew her ladyship for a couple of months, but I liked her very much, and I know you loved her. What kind of friend would I be if I didn't come to be with you now? For although our betrothal may be a sham, our friendship isn't."

Remembering the promise he had made to his grandmother, Tommy would have liked to tell her there and then that he regarded the betrothal as anything but a sham, but those words failed him. Instead he drew her down beside him on the sofa and told her what had happened.

"I know now that she was ailing when I left for Portsmouth," he said in anguish. "How I wish I had ignored her wishes and gone up to see her. I shall never be able to forgive myself for being away when she needed me most."

He had such despair on his face that she instinctively put her arms around him and drew him close. He looked at her for a moment then, hesitantly at first, but with growing assurance, pressed his lips to hers, at the same time gathering her into a firm embrace. His kiss was firm but gentle, his arms strong, and when he touched the tip of his tongue to her parted lips, she felt a bolt of passion from her breast to her groin.

The embrace lasted no more than a minute, but for Cecilia it was as if time stood still. When at last they drew apart, she felt as if she had entered a different universe. She had never even been held by a man before, much less kissed. She was speechless.

Seeing her confusion, Tommy dropped his arms and said, "I'm sorry, Cecilia, I don't know what made me do that. Forgive me."

"N... no," she said, coming to her senses and shaking her head. "Nothing to forgive ... you ... you were very unhappy and you needed human contact. It was natural. I was just here, that's all. Could have been ... could have been anybody."

Tommy started to reply that it was much more than that, and that, indeed, it could not have been anyone but her, but, in face of her kind but unsentimental understanding of the situation, he did not know where to begin.

They sat for some minutes, side by side but not touching, both now staring into the fire lost in their own thoughts. He was wondering how he could bring his betrothed around to the idea that he actually wanted to marry her, and not just because he had promised his grandmother. She was re-living the kiss, both wanting him to do it again and fearful that he would.

At length he stirred and said with a little laugh, "I am forgetting my manners. May I offer you something? A glass of madeira? A cup of tea?"

"A cup of tea would be very nice, thank you," she replied as lightly as she could. "Then I should probably go. My aunt and uncle don't know where I am. I left as soon as I received your note and didn't tell anyone. Heaven knows what they would say if they looked for me and found me gone. Actually, I do know what they would say and it would be *thank heavens she's gone*. I make them very uncomfortable, you know."

"I can't imagine why," he replied, going to ring the bell. "You have been very comforting to me."

This was true. Although he had not meant to kiss her, he was glad he had. Strangely, it had comforted him. Cecilia was right. He *had* needed human contact, and she had provided it, without making a fuss or demanding an explanation. She really was a very calm woman.

They smiled at each other and were still smiling when the butler came in. Drinking their tea and madeira they talked of what arrangements would now have to be made. The funeral would take place within a week at Westminster Abbey, and there would be a period of mourning during which family members, and this need not include Cecilia, would not attend anything but the quietest and most intimate of parties. When she said of course she would wear mourning, and be only too glad to withdraw from social events, Tommy tried to persuade Cecilia to go back to Madame Clothilde for black gowns. But she declared she would simply have her day dresses dyed. By the time she was out of black gloves, she reasoned, she would have achieved her financial independence and be able to set up her school. She would no longer need pretty dresses; in fact, black would be most suitable for her new situation.

She seemed so determined on her course of action that Tommy wondered how on earth he was going to manage to keep his promise to his grandmother. He hoped that somehow a way would suggest itself.

In the event, matters were taken out of his hands. He was at first surprised to receive a note from his grandmother's man of business asking him to invite Miss Beaumaris to the reading of the Will, which would take place at Broome House after the funeral baked meats. It was most unusual to include anyone but immediate family at such a moment, but Tommy assumed that Cecilia had perhaps been left an important item of jewelry, of which his grandmother had several pieces. Knowing how these things go in families, she would have wanted the bequest to be known to all, lest there be questions afterwards. He conveyed the message to Cecilia, who was as surprised as he, but willingly agreed to attend.

In the previous century it had been uncommon for women to attend funerals, it being considered that they had done more than their duty in attending the sick and dying. None but the lowest class of female would in any case follow the body to the burial site. Nowadays, however, it was increasingly seen as a mark of respect and even Christian duty to go to the funeral of close family members and important people. The Abbey was therefore filled to capacity for the Dowager's obsequies. The Allenby name was an ancient one, and both the older and younger scions of all the great families were there.

Cecilia's aunt, next to whom she was seated, constantly craned her neck to see and whisper the name of the attendees, each, it seemed, more august than the one before. It was the first time that Cecilia had given any serious thought to the social importance of her faux-betrothed and she found it hard to reconcile her laughing Tommy with the head of so important a family. She could see his golden waves against the black bonnets of the women on either side of him. One was obviously his sister Mariah, wearing a plain veiled hat on her flaxen hair. Then, next to her was a gentleman whom Cecilia recognized as her husband, Lord Chesterford. On Tommy's other side was a woman who gave the impression of being older than he. She was also fair and wore a number of veils over a flat-crowned bonnet. That must be his sister Eugenia, whose husband was Ambassador to Austria. Next to her sat a somewhat portly, balding man, the Ambassador himself, probably.

The coffin stood in front of the altar steps, draped in a flag-like cloth bearing the family crest. The name Allenby was embroidered beneath in gold. The coffin was surrounded by sheaves of white lilies whose scent perfumed the air. Once it seemed everyone was seated, an orchestra seated in the choir began to play a piece of music that Cecilia found out afterwards was Haydn's "Sad" Symphony no. 44. It began with a triumphant soaring of violins that gave way to muted instruments playing in a minor key. It was intensely moving.

However, this was disturbed near the beginning by a sudden craning of necks and the whole congregation rising to its feet as the Prince Regent and his brother, the Duke of Clarence, entered the Abbey. It no doubt confirmed the two princes in their own importance as they stumped ponderously down the aisle to the sounds of the glorious violins, but Cecilia was disgusted by their thoughtlessness. Then their arrival caused no little shifting and re-arrangement of seats, it being unthinkable that they should sit anywhere but in the front pew. Fortunately, everyone had settled down by the time the moving, elegiac movement was played and the orchestra fell silent.

When the music died away, the service began with an acclamation and prayer. Tommy read from the scriptures *Then we who are alive, who are left, will be caught up together with them in the clouds to meet the Lord ..."*. His handsome face was drawn and solemn but his voice did not shake. He held his head up and his vivid blue eyes were clear even from where she sat, several rows back. She now saw that he was every inch the head of a great family, brought up to show complete self-control in public. His voice never wavered, though she knew how deeply the death of his grandmother had affected him. Then the gentleman she took to be the Ambassador talked about the long life of the Dowager Countess and the central rock she had been to her family, especially in these last years, after the death of Tommy's parents. The congregation sang *Guide Me O Thou Great Jehovah*, and finally came the Commendation.

The congregation rose as Tommy, the Ambassador, Lord Chesterford and three other men she did not recognize shouldered the coffin and bore it slowly down the aisle and out of the church. The orchestra started up again, a joyful, soaring piece that Cecilia later learned was the final movement of the symphony they had begun before. It seemed a fitting ending for the willful but loving matriarch. Before the music had finished, the two Princes rose and processed in a stately fashion back down the aisle, so that the violins again appeared to be playing especially for them and the congregation was forced, once more, to rise. Cecilia turned her head away as they passed.

Back at Broome House, it was some time before Tommy returned from the burial and even longer before it was possible for him and the other family members to meet in the library for the reading of the Will. Mariah presented Cecilia to her older sister, and she made what conversation she could with her supposed future sisters-in-law. She was struck to the quick, however, by the ever-vivacious Mariah pointing out an overdressed lady in the crowd. In addition to black plumes on her bonnet, she wore rows of jet beads over a gown displaying a king's ransom in black lace.

"That Lady Peabody, she hated Grandmother!" she said in a loud whisper. "Look at her simpering sympathy! Lord Peabody was completely done up and married her for her money, apparently. She's the daughter of a rich merchant. Granny said that wouldn't matter a bit except that she gives herself such airs. It's all right to smell of the shop, Granny used to say, so long as you don't try to cover it up with French scent! She hated a fraud!"

Cecilia's heart dropped when she heard those words and she almost confessed her own fraud, but fortunately, the gentlemen arrived and the moment passed.

At length only a few guests remained, mostly gentlemen, who appeared to be stuck over the brandy in the smoking room. The family members trooped into the library, Cecilia lingering behind until Tommy took her hand with a squeeze and led her to one of the wide-bottomed oak armchairs that seemed to be the peculiar furnishings of most family libraries, here arranged in a vague semi-circle. A gentleman who was clearly the family lawyer, to judge from his rather old and unfashionable rusty black skirted coat over black knee-britches and stockings, took his place in front of the semi-circle and gestured to Tommy.

"I have put your place here, my lord," he said, indicating a more throne-like armchair set more or less in the center.

"Thank you, Cummings, but I shall remain here, next to Miss Beaumaris. Moorhouse, Mr. Ambassador, why don't you sit there? It suits you better than me."

Muttering self-deprecatory comments, but clearly glad to be placed, as it were, in the High Chair, Eugenie's husband moved from where he was sitting and took the seat indicated.

"The Will I am reading today," began the lawyer, placing his pince-nez on the end of his nose, "is one that her ladyship desired me to make just two days before she died."

There was a murmur at this, since the disposition of the Dowager's estate, such as was not entailed to the family, was considered a known quantity and long settled. Tommy was to inherit her personal fortune, and her granddaughters had been promised her jewelry. Her house, as everyone knew, was not hers personally, it had been purchased by Tommy's father out of the family estate when she refused to remove to the Dower House at Thyford. It therefore came back to the estate. There would be bequests of a minor nature, of course, but no one there expected any surprises.

"I should say at once," continued the lawyer, "that her ladyship was in perfect control of her faculties and there can be no doubt that the dispositions made in the Will were her choice, and hers alone."

He then went on to confirm, that with the exception of the bequests that would be read presently, the whole of the Dowager Lady Broome's personal fortune was bestowed, unreservedly, upon her grandson, The Lord Thomas Algernon Wymering Allenby, fourth Earl of Broome.

"For," she had dictated, "in spite of the silliness we often observe in him but which I believe to be a complete affectation, he is a good boy and I trust him absolutely. Although I would not have told him to his face while I was alive, he is the finest of three generations of Allenbys."

Tommy looked down at his hands, and Cecilia, seeing he was having to make a superhuman effort to hold back tears, took one of them and held it. The lawyer hurried on.

"To my granddaughters Eugenie and Mariah, I leave my jewelry for them to share as they see fit, with the exception of my gold-backed cameo with diamonds that I bequeath to Cecilia Beaumaris, as being the most suitable adornment for a schoolteacher."

Cecilia caught her breath. She had not expected such generosity or such thoughtfulness from Tommy's grandmother. And how had she known her plans? Had Tommy told her? But the lawyer had not finished.

"As far as my other jewels are concerned, I would, however, ask my granddaughters to confer with Tommy about what best becomes each of them. He is the only one of you with any taste."

Naturally enough, the two women looked askance at this suggestion but the normally quiet Lord Chesterford spoke up unexpectedly.

"She's right, y'know. Always thought she was the best turned out woman in the family, until Miss Beaumaris, of course." He smiled at Cecilia.

Mariah frowned and exclaimed, "Well I never ..." then saw Cecilia blushing and said with a shrug, "Oh, what's the use? We all know it's true!"

Cecilia had had her day gowns dyed, and she was wearing one now. She was one of the rare dark-haired women who look good in black. It seemed to bring out the unusual gold flecks in her eyes. The gown itself had the remarkable fit and drape of

Madame Clothilde's genius, and with her height, it was true that the funeral gown looked extremely elegant. Mariah's remark served to defuse the emotion of the moment and there was general subdued laughter.

The lawyer, who maintained a stony silence until the laughter died down, cleared his throat and declared, "There follow the bequests for the Dowager's long-standing servants, which I believe his lordship is already well aware of," Tommy nodded. "But two days before her death, her ladyship desired me to add one more." There was a stir of interest from the group. "I shall read it now." He cleared his throat again and took a deep breath. "To Miss Cecilia Beaumaris I bequeath the sum of fifteen thousand pounds to be realized from redeeming those placements that Mr. Cummings, in consultation with my grandson Tommy, shall deem appropriate. This sum, which shall be hers absolutely, is to be used in the formation and maintenance of the school for impoverished females that she is desirous of establishing. This bequest is, however, wholly dependent upon her marrying my grandson Tommy within three months of the date of my death. I do not wish the consideration of mourning to interfere with the celebration of this wedding. Everyone knows I intensely dislike black gloves anyway. Seeing Tommy suitably married will be a greater mark of honor to me than any period of mourning."

There was a collective indrawing of breath and everyone's head swiveled in the direction of Cecilia. She herself looked utterly dazed. She looked around, saying disjointedly, "But I don't ... it isn't ... however did ..." then rose so suddenly to her feet that her chair tipped over backwards, and gasping, "I'm sorry ... please forgive ... I can't ..." she ran out of the room.

Tommy, who had stood up holding out his hand towards her before her precipitate departure, turned to the rest of the company. "I must go after her. I think we are at the end in any case?" He looked enquiringly at the lawyer, who nodded. "Please stay and enjoy the hospitality of Broome House as long as you like."

Then he strode rapidly to the door, stopping only to take the greatcoat and hat that the butler thrust into his hands, calling for his carriage to be brought around and follow him. He was going after Miss Beaumaris.

Chapter Fourteen

Hardly knowing what she was doing, Cecilia had run through the hall, wrenched open the front door and almost fallen onto the street outside. In a walk so rapid it was almost a run, she set off down the street, not thinking at all about where she was going, oblivious to the curious looks of those she passed. In fact, there were not many people in the streets that evening. The fine weather of autumn had turned to an early winter. The day on which the Dowager Lady Broome had been soaked to the skin was the first of a period of biting wind and piercing rain showers. Cecilia gradually became aware that a fine snow was falling, and that in her haste, she had entirely forgotten to pick up her cloak and her bonnet. She had not wanted to dye the lovely silk shawl her aunt had given her, so she had no shawl either.

Droplets of freezing water running down the back of her neck brought her fully to her senses and she stopped her raging stride to look around and see where she was. She did not know the area at all well, since Tommy lived alone, and for propriety's sake she had only been there once or twice before. She now saw that she had come down towards the Thames and wondered which turn to take to get to Bruton Street. She knew it could not be all that far away. As she hesitated with indecision, she noticed a pile of rags in the doorway of one of the tall buildings lining the street. The pile of rags moved and a pale, thin hand reached out to her.

"Please Miss," came a reedy voice, "can yer 'elp my baby?"

Cecilia went closer and bending over the form, saw to her horror that there lay a girl who could not have been more than fourteen, clutching a bundle of grey cloth that she now thrust towards her.

"Take my baby, Miss, I begs yer. Don't worry 'bout me, but she's so cold. I ain't bin able to feed 'er these last two days. Can yer take 'er and warm 'er up and give 'er sumthin?"

Without thinking, Cecilia took the bundle, which weighed no more than the thin cloth itself, and as she moved the folds apart, she beheld a sight that would be seared on her memory for the rest of her life. A dead baby lay there, as grey as the filthy cloths it was bound in, its little face wizened like a tiny monkey. Cecilia gave a great sob and clutched it to her own breast, cold and drenched as she now was, as if by some primal force she could urge the life from her own heart back into the child.

At that moment, a figure came up behind her, and she saw, to her immense relief, that it was Tommy. Mutely, she handed the grey bundle to him and then turned back to the girl who still lay on the ground. She tried to help her up, but the girl had no strength left, and could barely get to her knees. Cecilia knelt down and tried to pick the girl up, but she was so hampered by her wet gown and her hands were so cold, that she could not. Then she felt a strong hand on her arm as Tommy helped her to her feet, gave her back the baby and scooped the girl up from the ground.

She had been so intent upon the plight of the young mother that she was not aware a carriage had arrived until Tommy mounted the steps and placed his human bundle on the seat, then turned, took the baby from her and lay next to its mother.

Then he handed her up the steps, and, having said a word to the driver, finally got in himself.

"Can't take her to Broome House," he said as the driver whipped up the horses, "Too many people still there. Taking her to m'grandmother's. The housekeeper will know what to do."

He took off his great coat and wrapped it around Cecilia, whose teeth were by now chattering so hard that she could not utter a word. He then bent across to the opposite bench and put his hand on the young mother, who lay motionless.

"Taking you somewhere warm, Madam," he said softly. "You and your baby. No need for you to worry."

There was an almost imperceptible lessening of the tension in the figure under the rags. Though she was still shivering with cold, Cecilia unwrapped herself from the greatcoat and lay it on the two inert figures. Tommy made as if to protest, but then, without a word, stripped off his black superfine jacket and placed it over her shoulders.

"B...but T...Tommy!" she stuttered, trying to give it back, "y...you will b...be c...cold, a... and y...your c...coat w...will be r...ruined!"

"If I may put my arms around you, you will keep me warm, and I don't give a damn about the coat," he smiled at her.

"I'm t...too c...cold t...to keep y...you w...warm, b...but I...I'd like y...your a...arms a...around me."

So Tommy held her tight and she put her head against his shoulder. She was relaxing in his embrace until she suddenly remembered the reason why she had dashed off in such a way, without her cloak or her bonnet. She was cast into confusion again by the shock of the bequest and, still more, its prerequisite. Her wild thoughts were interrupted by a murmur from the young woman, though, when Cecilia bent over to look at her, her eyes were still closed. There was no time now to think about her own predicament, she said to herself. Here they were dealing with life and death.

They were soon at the Dowager's house and Tommy was explaining the situation to Mobley. That individual had known Tommy since his youth and was more or less immune to his pranks and peculiarities. But even he was shocked to see his lordship in shirtsleeves in the snow, though still with his tall hat on his head, his betrothed with his coat wrapped over her sodden gown, her drenched hair falling from its pins, clutching what looked like a bundle of rags, and a groom carrying what appeared to be a body of a girl swathed in the Earl's greatcoat.

He immediately sent for the housekeeper, judging it women's business, best dealt with by that cheerful soul. Mrs. Robinson bustled them all downstairs into a warm servants' parlor, where the young mother was laid on a sofa, and immediately dismissed his lordship, with his greatcoat. She would have dismissed Miss Beaumaris, but that lady, in quiet but firm tones, declared she felt responsible for the young mother and anyway, she was in no condition to be above stairs in her bedraggled state. She allowed the housekeeper to take the bundle from her arms. No explanation was needed for her to see that the baby was dead.

The housekeeper bore the child away and returned a little later with a voluminous wool dressing gown. It had been worn, she explained, by the late Earl in his old age, as he had felt the cold. It was the only thing she could think of that would cover Miss Beaumaris's ankles. Not a single gown in the house would be long enough. If Miss would like to remove her wet things, they could be dried and ironed. She could not stay in them, for she would catch her death of cold. Since she had given Tommy back his damp coat, Cecilia was shivering again and knew what Mrs. Robinson said was true. So she went into a corner and stripped off her wet things, wrapping herself in the scratchy wool garment she had been given.

By this time, the young mother was stirring and calling plaintively for her baby. Cecilia knelt by her and explained gently that the child was dead.

"I tried to keep 'er warm," whispered the poor girl in a broken voice, her throat full, "but it's bin so cold an' we dint 'ave nowhere to go." She had to stop for breath. "They threw me out when they found I were in the family way, even though, "she stopped again, "it were the young master's child." Her chest heaved and she clasped Cecilia's arm. "Can I see her?" she whispered.

Mrs. Robinson nodded and went outside, returning with the baby, who had been washed and was now wrapped in a clean linen cloth. She handed the child to her mother.

"At least she won't 'ave to suffer no more," said the girl in a low voice, kissing the child. "That's all we women 'ave to look forward to: sufferin'." And she lay back on the sofa, exhausted, her throat gurgling.

"Let me take her, now, dear," said Mrs. Robinson to the young mother. "We'll make the arrangements. Let me give you a wash and put some dry things on you, then you'll have some warm broth. You'll soon feel better. What's your name, and the baby's?"

"I'm Lizzy and she's Ivy," whispered the girl. "I called 'er that coz she 'eld ever so tight to my finger the minute she were born. Ivy, she is."

The housekeeper disappeared with the baby, reappearing a few minutes later with a bowl of broth and a bundle of clothing.

"Do you go upstairs, now, Miss," she said to Cecilia. "We'll look after her. I've had a fire built in one of the bedrooms and she'll be carried up there. His lordship has been asking after you. You'd best go to him. He won't mind the old dressing gown, for all he's so smart himself!"

Cecilia knew this was true, so, after smoothing the young mother's brow and murmuring that everything would be all right, she went upstairs to Tommy.

He was sitting in the library, a room that had been rarely used since his grandfather's time. It still smelled faintly, but not unpleasantly, of tobacco. A fire had been lit and the long red curtains drawn, and it looked cozy. Tommy was sitting in a wing chair with his stockinged feet up on the fender. When he saw Cecilia, he rose to his feet, smiling ruefully.

"Please forgive my lack of boots. Mobley took them away to try to save them. I feel damnably undressed without them! But if you can stand the sight of my feet, come and sit by the fire."

Cecilia smiled. "Compared with the appearance I must make in an old dressing gown of your grandfather's, your lack of boots pales into insignificance. I very nearly didn't come upstairs at all. But it was obvious Mrs. Robinson wanted me out of the way, so here I am." She sat in a wing chair opposite him. "Try not to look below my neck — although above my neck is not much better. I know my hair is all falling down but if I put it up in a knot it is so thick, it will never dry. In fact, would you mind if I took it down completely?"

The tendrils of hair that had fallen down were drying into curls all around her face, making her look much younger and more vulnerable, and the dressing gown, which had been wrapped twice around her and tied tightly at her waist, accentuated her shape. Tommy found it hard to obey the stricture not to look below her neck, especially as he had the impression she was all but naked underneath the woolly garment. She looked more desirable than any woman he had ever laid eyes on.

"I wish you would," he said. "I know that girls are supposed to mark the transition into womanhood by putting up their hair, but any man will tell you it's a damned shame." He looked at her appreciatively. Then, collecting himself, he went to a small table at the side of the room, coming back with a wide bottomed glass containing an amber liquid. "Here, drink this. Brandy. It'll warm you up. Mobley said Cook was making some soup and I told him to serve it in here. I didn't think either of us would feel like sitting in the dining room."

Murmuring thanks, Cecilia took the glass, and sipped tentatively. The brandy felt like a river of fire going down her throat, and although she did not exactly like it, it did make her feel wonderfully warm. She sat, sipping occasionally, slowly taking the remaining pins out of her hair and running her fingers through it. She was glad of something to do, knowing they would have to talk, sooner or later, about the extraordinary bequest from the Dowager Lady Broome.

"Cecilia …", began Tommy, at the same time as she said, "Tommy …."

They both stopped and laughed self-consciously.

Then Tommy said, "Ladies first …" and waited for her to continue.

She took a deep breath. "I'm sorry I acted as I did when that shocking bequest was read. It was not only rude but also cowardly. But oh, Tommy!" she exclaimed, "What am I to do? I don't want to marry you for the sake of your grandmother's money, and I'm sure you don't want me as a wife under any circumstances, much less under those! But seeing that young woman convinces me still more that something must be done to help these poor girls. She can't be more than fourteen! She's only a child herself and was apparently seduced by the son of the household then thrown out. It's inhuman!"

Tommy leaned forward and took her hand. She had never seen him look so serious. "Put aside for the moment my feelings about you marrying me for my money, and let me ask you this. Do you think living with me and having enough money to set up your school would be worse than living in a hovel and constantly worrying if you can afford it? And by living with me I mean precisely that. I would place no … demands upon you that you did not feel you could …" he hesitated, "reciprocate."

Cecilia looked him straight in the eye. "You mean we would not have to …."

"Exactly. We would not have to."

"But the whole point of your grandmother's bequest was to make me marry you so there would be an heir. She must have guessed that the betrothal is a sham."

"Yes, I've thought about that. She was a shrewd old lady, but let's worry about that later. For now, you just have to think about how you may achieve your goal." His eyes twinkled and he was back to his normal self. "I remember learnin' somethin' about that at Eton. Amazin' what comes back to you when you least expect it. One of the old Beaks used to say it all the time: *happiness and freedom begin with one principle. Some things are within your control and some are not.* 'Course, he was talking about avoiding prep, which I always used to try to do and kept gettin' flogged for it. *Not within your control, Allenby,* he used to say *and you'll be miserable until you learn what is.*"

He looked lost in thought for a moment. "He was right, of course. Well, my dear, setting up your school is within your control and if that will make you happy, I for one, say it's worth marrying me to do it."

Cecilia could not help but smile at him. He seemed to have the ability to make the most difficult things simple. But it was not simple.

"But what about you? Won't you feel … *used*? I mean, I would literally be marrying you for money. The very thing I scorned all those men for when they offered me marriage thinking I was rich!"

Tommy hesitated, then said, "You wouldn't be marrying me for my money. It's my grandmother's! I'm not giving you a penny, well, not unless you ask for it, and I know you won't. Good lord! You won't even let me buy you a trumpery dress! Come to think of it, that will have to change. You'll have to have all your personal bills sent to me. Not your professional expenses, of course, just your personal ones. New bonnets, gloves, that sort of thing. I'll like that. I can take you to task over spending too much on fripperies. Make me feel like a real husband." He smiled at her, his eyes laughing.

Cecilia had to smile back and was about to protest that she never bought fripperies, but at that moment Mobley came in carrying a large silver tray, on which was placed a steaming tureen of something smelling delicious, two bowls, a loaf of bread and some butter.

"Cook's compliments, my lord," said Mobley. "She trusts this will be satisfactory. Her ladyship no longer … er being with us, the kitchen is not fully stocked." He placed the tray on a side table. "Would you want me to be serving you, your lordship?"

"No thanks, Mobley. We'll serve ourselves. And thank Cook for us, won't you? It smells delicious."

The butler bowed and then said "Oh, Miss, Mrs. Robinson says as how the young … er person is comfortable in one of the back bedchambers and she can convey you there before you go, if you was wanting. Your garments will be dry presently and she will have them pressed. He left, quietly shutting the door behind him.

"Shall I bring you a bowl of soup?" asked Cecilia, preparing to get up.

"Not yet. I intend to starve you into submission. No soup for you until you agree to Grandmother's terms, and mine, come to that. You marry me, then you spend her money and your own on your school. I spend my money on you and no argument."

Cecilia was quiet for a moment, then she said, "Very well, if you're sure that's what you want. This day has been so upsetting I honestly don't know what I want."

"Then we shall do this the correct way," announced Tommy, rising to his feet. "Stand up, please."

She stood. He went down on one knee before her and took her hand. "Miss Beaumaris, will you do me the honor of accepting my name in marriage?"

Cecilia looked down at him. "Yes, Mr. Allenby. I will. But please stand up. All this formal convention seems ridiculous when I'm standing here in an old dressing gown and you are in your stockings."

"Formal convention is there for a reason, my dear," he said, rising. "It brings with it a sense of officialdom so that you may never say I didn't offer for you in due form. Now, I believe convention also dictates that I may kiss my betrothed. That's the other good thing about it."

He put his arms around her and pulled her close. He had not held her since the evening of his grandmother's death, except for earlier in the carriage, when they were both just trying to keep warm. She had so rarely been enclosed in anyone's arms in her life. Her parents had not been demonstrative people and she had never been allowed to get to know any of her nannies well enough. Miss Warren, her friend and mentor, had held her for a moment now and then, usually as they left or greeted one another, but it was nothing like this. She could not believe how wonderful it was to feel so sheltered, so protected.

Then he placed his warm, soft lips on hers and she found herself responding to his kiss in a way that took her by surprise. This time, his tongue came fully into her mouth and the same bolt shot through her as before. When they broke apart, her heart was hammering and her breath came in gasps. She did not know if she wanted him to stop or to continue.

Tommy broke the silence. "Although we are not going to … well, consummate our marriage in the usual way," he said, smiling at her, "I hope I may kiss you from time to time. Especially if you continue to wear that dressing gown. I really find it quite irresistible." His eyes danced.

"What humbug!" said Cecilia, relieved that the tension had been diffused. "How can you, Tommy Allenby, the best-dressed man in London, find a scratchy old wool thing like this irresistible?"

"Even the best of us have occasional lapses in judgement," he replied lightly, thinking it best not to say it was not the dressing gown, but what was underneath it, that he found so alluring.

"May we have our soup now, before it gets cold?" asked the ever-practical Miss Beaumaris, "and then we had best find our clothes and go home. And I do want to look in on Lizzy – the young woman, that's her name. I hope everyone hasn't waited for us at Broome House, by the way."

"Yes, I suppose we should go," sighed Tommy regretfully, much more the romantic at heart. "Hot soup and dry boots. Nanny would approve. But don't worry about the rest of the family. I sent a note round to say I had found you and was taking you home. The footman brought back your cloak and bonnet, by the way."

"Oh Tommy! You think of everything," said Miss Beaumaris, picking up the soup ladle.

They drank their soup and ate their bread and butter sitting opposite each other in the wing chairs by the fire, for all the world like an old married couple. Tommy thought once again how restful she was. She did not fidget or demand. She was entirely unselfconscious. Her hair dried into a mass of tangled curls, but apart from pushing it behind her ears from time to time, she did not bother with it. When her fingers became buttery, she sucked them unconcernedly, until Tommy, who found the whole procedure almost more provocative than he could stand, gave her yet another of his snow-white handkerchiefs.

She talked about how she would tell Mr. Davis that he could set his mind at rest about her setting up her school in the very worst part of London. When Tommy remarked that she would be coming to live with him in Broome House, she answered, "yes, of course," in an entirely abstracted fashion, so that he felt he could have said they were to live on the moon, and she would have agreed. He sighed inwardly, realizing that now she had agreed to the necessity of marrying him in order to access his grandmother's bequest, her whole attention was on her school. He was very far down the list of importance. He hoped his grandmother, wherever she was, was happy.

Chapter Fifteen

This proved to be very much the case. Cecilia spent the time between the reading of the Will and the wedding organizing her new school. She contacted Mr. Davis telling him about the bequest. With more money to invest, her monthly revenue would be increased by at least two-thirds, so she could afford larger premises and hopefully not in the absolute worst neighborhoods. This would now be necessary, she realized, not for the teaching area but for lodging the staff. Now she herself would not be able to live on the premises, she would need a housekeeper. She had always intended to hire a second teacher, possibly one who could teach sewing and the other domestic arts she could not, so she would definitely need several bedchambers. For she could not forget Bridget, whom she was determined to take with her.

Mr. Davis therefore spread his net a little wider and came up with a property on the corner of Chapel Street in the East End, far enough away from the docks to avoid the foul air and most of the unsavory population clustered there, but not so far as to be inaccessible to pupils. It was nonetheless an impoverished area and a very far cry from the stately homes of Mayfair. Men and women in grimy clothes with furtive expressions hung around in doorways, though when Cecilia smiled and nodded to them, they most often nodded back. A couple approached her with outstretched hands, but when she said "I'm sorry, I have nothing to give you," they left her alone.

It was a three-story property with the distinct advantage of being at the other end of the street from the public house that was a feature of nearly every corner in the East End. Being on the corner, it was larger than the other houses in the street. It was also joined to a single-story building between it and the next house. This gave the impression of having been a shop at some time, since next to the front door there was a large display window. Around the corner there was another front door flanked by a more normal size window. Cecilia judged this to have been the access to the dwelling, while the other door would have opened into the shop, the single-story building being some sort of warehouse.

The house had been uninhabited for some time and was both malodorous, damp and extremely dirty, besides being infested with vermin. Downstairs, the shop door opened into a long, narrow room with a door at the bottom leading into a large kitchen and scullery. The side building proved to be a single large room with a coal hole in one corner. Scraps of yellowed and brittle paper bearing hand lettered words like *Dry'd Pees* and *Britannia Sugar* lay on the floor, confirming that the space had at one time been used for food storage. The window onto the street had been boarded up, but a back window looked out onto the yard.

The living space on the other side of the house was accessed off the kitchen and proved to be made up of two rooms downstairs, and two more off each of the first and second landings. They were all stained from a leaking roof and were chillingly cold and uninviting, the walls moldy and discolored. However, all the rooms had fireplaces and the kitchen had a large open hearth. The chimneys would, of course, need to be cleaned and examined. However, there was ample living accommodation for at least four people, while the storage area would make a good schoolroom.

The scullery gave onto a back yard with a water pump and a privy, disgustingly filthy. But there was also a garden, now overgrown and rank. It was all in a dreadful condition, but there was nothing here, Cecilia decided, that could not be cleaned and fixed, and with the introduction of a good cat, the vermin problem could hopefully be overcome.

The biggest problem, she thought, was that women living in this neighborhood without male protection would feel insecure. She hated to admit it, but they would need a man on the premises. But, determined that this and any other problem could and would be overcome, she asked Mr. Davis to pursue negotiations with the owners, telling him not to mention who she was, and certainly not give Tommy's name, since that would undoubtedly raise the price. He should concentrate on the dilapidated state of the premises and the fact that without a considerable amount being spent on it, it was uninhabitable.

In the midst of this, she did not fail to visit Lizzy, whom the doctor had diagnosed with inflammation of the lungs, not unlike that which had carried off the Dowager. She was very poorly for several days, but by dint of burning pastilles in her room, keeping her warm and feeding her a nourishing broth, Mrs. Robinson pulled her through. Cecilia visited as often as she could and often surprised the two of them talking together much like mother and daughter.

Details of Lizzy's life emerged little by little. She had lost her mother to consumption when she was eleven, and had spent the next three years doing her best to keep house for her two older brothers and her father. The two boys had finally left home and her father had found a new wife who, with daughters of her own, had no intention of allowing Lizzy to remain with them.

She was a pretty little thing and because of her abilities in the kitchen, honed by her years of keeping house for her father and brothers, she had had little trouble in finding employment as a kitchen maid in a middle-class household. These were common in the commercial areas of London to the west of St. Paul's.

All had been well until her prettiness had caught the eye of the son of the house, with the consequences known to them all. When she had become pregnant, not only had the owners of the house in which she worked thrown her out, but her stepmother had refused to give her shelter, shrilly accusing her of being a whore.

Mrs. Robinson was a childless woman in her forties and, unusually for a housekeeper, was actually married. Her husband had been a soldier during the great engagements with Bonaparte. He had been wounded in the foot, and the resulting limp had ended his military career. The Dowager had taken him into her household when he was discharged from the army, and he acted as a general factotum, lifting and carrying and doing general repairs.

Tommy had, however, decided to sell his grandmother's house. He could not see a use for it. The estate already possessed the Dower house her ladyship had declined to use. Both his sisters had married the inheritors of family homes of their own, and he and Cecilia were to live, naturally enough, in Broome House. Mobley and Cook were to be given a pension and cottages on the estate, the footmen and maids would either be absorbed into the households of the rest of the family or given references for new employment.

The Robinsons were a harder case to settle, until Cecilia came into the room one day and heard her saying to Lizzy, "Try not to take it so hard, my dear. You're young and pretty," for now she was feeling better, the girl's sweet, dimpled face was filling out. "You'll be married one day and have more babies, just wait and see. I was unlucky that way. The little ones never came. I always thought I'd like to be around children, but there you are, you do what you can, and I ended up housekeeping."

It was as if a bolt from heaven came to Cecilia. "If you would like to work with children," she said excitedly, and if you can stand living in the East End, "would you and Mr. Robinson consider working in my little school?"

"Lord bless you, Miss," answered the housekeeper, "I come from the East End myself, for all that I studied to lose the cockney, as I believe they call it. I had to, for my job. My husband Bill too, we were both born within the sound of Bow Bells. If you listen to him speak, you'll hear it right enough. Now, as for your school, I've heard you mention it, Miss. I don't know as I could be a teacher, except in teaching how to keep a household. I've done enough of that over the years, with the housemaids."

"But that is exactly what I need! You and your husband are the answer to my prayers!" Cecilia explained the situation and added, "And you, too, Lizzy! I'll need someone who can cook simple but plentiful meals, if you don't mind going back to where you came from."

"Oh, no, Miss! I was happy enough wiv me Dad and me bruvvers, only when that woman come, she din't want none of me, so I 'ad to go away. But I likes that part of London. I knows me way around."

Thus it was agreed that Mrs. Robinson, or Robbie, as that lady begged Cecilia, like Tommy, to call her, would speak to her husband about the jobs for them both. Lizzy said she would go anywhere Robbie went, even if it meant working in a midden.

"Oh, I don't think it will come to that!" laughed Cecilia, "Though the property might at the moment be compared not unreasonably to a midden."

If they had been surprised with the intelligence that Cecilia was intending to open a school in the East End and that the Dowager both knew of it and supported it, the rest of the family were not at all surprised when Tommy announced he and Miss Beaumaris would be married at the end of the following month, just six weeks after the funeral. They had all heard the terms of the late Lady Broome's bequest, and although it was highly irregular, they did not blame Cecilia for accepting it. After all, they said to themselves, she was already betrothed to Tommy. She would have married him sooner or later.

No announcement was made in the papers, since it was felt that only by revealing family affairs could anyone understand so unusual a happening. In any case, her mind entirely absorbed in her educational plans, never has any bride been less interested in the details of her wedding than Cecilia Beaumaris. When her sisters-in-law or aunt, who were the only women who knew about the upcoming nuptials, interrogated her about her wedding clothes, she answered them vaguely or with a shake of her head. In fact, it was Tommy who saw Madame Clothilde and decided on a pale lilac gown with a silver-grey long-trained lace overdress for his fiancée, declaring that his bride would not wear black, no matter how deep in mourning they might be.

"Dammit," he said, "she'd look as if she were joining a cloister. I may rate myself pretty high, but she ain't goin' to be the bride of Christ!"

The only stipulation Cecilia did make was that she would prefer to be married in the church of St. Mary Magdalene in Old Fish Street, where she had gone to Sunday services with the other boarders at Mrs. Farridge's establishment. It was a fine old church rebuilt after the Great Fire of London by Sir Christopher Wren, or, at least, by his associates.

As a very little girl she had never been taken to church, since her parents found religion, like so many other things, unscientific and useless. She was first taken to St. Mary's by her friend Miss Warren and liked its dim, close interior. There were tall windows, to be sure, but they were set high up in the walls and the little light fell dustily on the congregation below. It was a foreshortened rectangle that made it look almost square, with a squat little tower on top, built that way, apparently, so as not to compete with the spire of St. Paul's a little way away. The interior featured some quite lovely stone carving that held the girl's interest, even when the sermons did not. There was an old brass plaque set in the floor pronouncing *How smale soever the gift shall be, Thanke God for him who gave it thee*, a sentiment that the young girl, who had rarely received a gift in her life, heartily agreed with.

It was to this church, therefore, that she was transported with her aunt and uncle, in the old-fashioned emblazoned Broome carriage on the morning of her wedding. She looked very lovely in her lilac and silver gown with its long train. Her aunt had exclaimed over the yards of lace required for the overdress and train and Cecilia's veil.

"Point d'Alençon lace, my dear! Acres of it! Must have cost a king's ransom!"

"Oh, don't say that, aunt, please!" cried Cecilia. "It quite destroys my pleasure to think Tommy spent so much money on a gown I may wear only once!"

"Nonsense! That modiste of yours will be able to change it up into something else, have no fear. You're too like your mother, Cecily … Cecilia. She would not spend a groat more than she had to on her clothing. But I declare, Thomas Allenby is the richest man in London. You may have anything you please."

"But that's just it, I don't please!" cried Cecilia. "When I think that this dress would probably pay the wages for my school for a year, it makes me ashamed!"

"Don't for heaven's sake say that to your husband," counseled her aunt. "If he wants to shower you with rich gifts, let him. I only wish I could say the same!"

She glanced at Cecilia's stolid uncle sitting next to her, but he pretended not to have heard the exchange. Cecilia herself just sighed.

They arrived at the church causing a stir, as the lumbering coach with its gold and blue crest disgorged the lovely bride and her two companions. Since no announcement had been in the papers and the family had been sworn to secrecy, the pews were nearly empty. Cecilia, who wrote every week to her friend Laura Warren, had invited her to her upcoming wedding, but without divulging the circumstances behind it. Miss Warren had replied with heartfelt congratulations, saying she had known all along that her protégée would find a husband, though even she had never envisaged an Earl! She regretted, however, that she did not feel up to making the trip to London as she was finding the slightest exertion brought on an asthma attack.

Apart from her aunt and uncle, therefore, the only people in the congregation were Tommy's two sisters and their husbands, and an older couple, sitting somewhat apart. Cecilia realized they must be Tommy's aunt from the North with the husband who had caused the family to cast her off. It was so like Tommy to have invited them, she thought.

Tommy had arranged for huge bouquets of white flowers at intervals along the aisle and in front of the altar, and they glowed in the dim interior of the church. The organ struck up a lovely piece of music as she walked slowly down the aisle, accompanied by her uncle. She did not know it and realized with a shock of guilt that she had not even been interested in the music for her own wedding. Her groom was waiting for her and smiled as he saw her in the dress he had chosen.

"Perfect, my dear," he said. "Just perfect."

He himself was, as always, equally perfect, in a swallow-tailed black coat with black britches, silk stockings and shining shoes. His waistcoat was silver grey, like her overdress. Tommy's friend Bunty, whom she had first met at Lady March's shooting weekend, was best man and stood behind him, very well dressed, but somehow lacking Tommy's elegance.

As they sat for the reading of the lessons and the sermon, Cecilia found herself looking around the old church. The lost little girl who had come here as a child and then left again as an equally lost young woman was setting out once more into uncharted waters. But this time, as she felt the touch of Tommy's shoulder against her own, she did not feel alone. Her heart felt curiously light and when the time came for the exchange of vows, she spoke up clearly, without a tremor in her voice. When the Vicar pronounced the solemn words: *I now pronounce you husband and wife and what therefore God hath joined together, let not man put asunder,* she and Tommy looked at each other and smiled.

The organ played the sound of trumpets as they walked back down the aisle, but, as they left the church, no bells rang. Cecilia remembered a conversation to which she had scarcely paid attention, when Tommy mentioned that, out of respect, he preferred to have no bells rung so soon after his grandmother's death. There were no rose petals scattered, and no crowds as they left the church. They merely stepped onto the workaday street of the city.

The few people wandering past stopped and gaped as the handsome couple came down the steps. Tommy put his hand in his pocket and withdrew a handful of gold coins, which he threw towards them, but by the time the small crowd had realized what was happening and word had begun to spread, Tommy and Cecilia had climbed into his carriage and were off. The others followed in the Broome coach or their own vehicles.

They all went to a wedding luncheon in a private room at Rules, organized, of course, by Tommy. His best man Bunty gave a somewhat incoherent speech in which, presumably to emphasize the point that his friend had at last found his one true love, he seemed to be prepared to enumerate all of Tommy's previous inamorata, until he received a sharp kick on the ankle from the groom. He then stopped abruptly, proposed the toast, sat down, and proceeded to drink champagne steadily the rest of the afternoon.

"Always was an idiot, even at Eton," laughed Tommy, his eyes twinkling at Cecilia, in no way discomposed by his friend. "But he means well. No better man in a tight corner, unless he's tight himself, of course, which he very often is. But there you are. A friend's a friend."

"I was finding it quite interesting, actually," said Cecilia. "I was wondering how you found time to fit so many of them in, if you see what I mean. Haven't you ever had anything else to do?"

Tommy, who indeed had rather a lot to do with the running of his huge estate and who, though he had a secretary, a business manager, an agent and a bailiff, often felt there were not enough hours in the day, laughed again.

"Not anythin' half so interestin', at any rate," he said. "But all that's behind me now. I'm a married man and my whole interest will be in promoting domestic felicity. I'll be pointed out as the model husband."

Cecilia had, in fact, given serious thought to the consequences of the odd marriage she and Tommy had engaged in. She had told herself it would be normal for him to seek elsewhere the embraces he was not to receive at home. She had chided herself for finding the idea disturbing, but it was not something they had ever discussed. Now she said quietly, "I would understand if you were not such a model husband. I am not exactly going to be a model wife."

He squeezed her hand and smiled at her, but said nothing.

The small party proved to be a very successful one, as the Ambassador and Cecilia's uncle found much in common, and Eugenie, who was inclined to act older than her years, found her aunt very compatible. Mariah pursued a lively, if silly, conversation with Bunty, whom she had known all her life. Cecilia found herself talking to Tommy's aunt Vera and her red-cheeked, good humored husband Lester, and then becoming involved in a conversation between Tommy, his uncle and Lord Chesterford.

Mariah's husband had inherited a highly encumbered estate, for his father had been an inveterate gambler and had left him with a mountain of debt. He seemed keenly interested in what Tommy had to say about farm management, about which, to Cecilia's surprise, Tommy seemed to know a great deal. It appeared that the late Lord Chesterford had not only done nothing but take money out of the estate, but had refused all attempts to introduce reforms.

"I can't help but think that if my father had listened to his agent, we might not be debt-free, God knows, but we might be doing better. But he just always said that if doing something one way was good enough for his father, it was good enough for him. But I'm more and more convinced he was way off the mark," said the young Chesterford, looking around apologetically.

"You're reet there," chipped in Uncle Lester in his north country accent. "There's no reason t'all to keep doing it all th' same when things've changed. Look at my cotton mills! We used t' have th'mules for the spinning machines, but now we use water power. Back in my Da's time they did it all b' hand. How d'yer think we would've survived if we'd kept on with that?"

Yes," agreed Tommy. "In my grandfather's day they used to leave twenty percent of the land fallow all the time to improve the yields, but when we started growing clover, we could both feed the cattle and improve the soil. Then we began growing turnips in the winter where before nothing grew. Personally, I'd rather starve than eat a turnip, but the cows like it well enough."

"What? You don't eat neeps?" bellowed Uncle Lester. "you're reet mistook, young man. Nothing better than neeps mashed oop with butter and tatties."

"Fie on you, Lester, you will have people thinking you eat like a peasant!" cried aunt Vera. "We most certainly do not eat such a thing!"

"More's the pity!" roared Lester, giving his wife a smacking kiss on the cheek. Then, turning to Cecilia, "You look here, Lady Broome! Do you give Lord Tommy plenty of neeps and tatties and you'll have young'uns running around yer knees in no time!"

Cecilia's face was scarlet, but Tommy just laughed, and said "Then lead me to them, my good man!"

When the party broke up, the afternoon was quite far advanced. Tommy's aunt and uncle were staying with the Chesterfords, who were young enough to know little or nothing about the family rift and not to care about it when they found out. In fact, Mariah was delighted with her uncle Lester who proved to be a devotee of modern conveniences. He at once gave the young couple all sorts of advice as to how to bring the gloomy kitchens of Chesterford House up to date and, indeed, improve the general efficiency of the whole place, which had remained unchanged for over fifty years. It certainly did not have gaslight, which a few of the larger London homes had recently installed. Her aunt and uncle were unfortunately childless, in spite, one might say, of the neeps and tatties, but by the time the stay was over, it was obvious that the Chesterfords were to become the offspring they never had.

After the animation of the luncheon party, Tommy and Cecilia were quiet in the carriage on the way to Broome House. Cecilia had been so involved with plans for her school that, not only had she ignored the wedding plans, but neither had she thought about what her new life might be like. Now, suddenly, it was borne in upon her that she would be Lady Broome, with a huge house in London and estates in the country she had never even seen. Tommy had said they would have to go into Middlesex to visit Thyford quite soon, for he must introduce the new Lady Broome, but they had not yet set a date. How was she going to reconcile her two lives? For his part, Tommy was wondering about the more immediate future. That night, in fact. He had told Cecilia he would not expect them to live as man and wife in the real sense, but now that it was upon them, it seemed less simple.

Cecilia's ordeal began the minute they were greeted at Broome House by the butler whom Cecilia knew from previous visits was called Preston.

"Welcome to Broome House, my lady," he intoned with enormous solemnity and led her towards the full complement of staff who stood in the hall to greet her: housekeeper, cook, footmen, upstairs maids, kitchen maids, boot boy and grooms. They all bowed and curtseyed as their lord and lady appeared. Preston presented the housekeeper, Mrs. Smithers, and the cook, Mrs. Wilkins, but declined to give the names of the underservants.

"What time would you wish dinner to be served, my lady?" asked Mrs. Smithers, "And may I presume you and his lordship will be dining alone this evening?"

Cecilia, who had given dinner not a single thought, looked in panic at Tommy. He answered lightly, "Oh, the usual time. Eight o'clock. And yes, it will be just the two of us."

They were led into the drawing room and at last left alone. They both sank thankfully into the wing chairs on either side of the fire. After a moment, Tommy smiled at her and asked,

"I don't wish to appear indelicate, but as our evening will not be following the accustomed formula for the first night of a marriage, I wonder if there is something else you'd like to do?"

Cecilia hesitated, then looked at him. "I'd like to talk about your grandmother's bequest, if I may." He nodded agreeably. "The thing is, I've found a property I believe will do quite well for the school. It's not, of course, in a very ... good neighborhood. Quite the reverse, in fact. And it needs a great deal of work to make it habitable. May I," she hesitated, "may I draw on the bequest immediately now we are married? I cannot use my own money until I am twenty-five, which is in two months, but I should really like to get started and I shall need a significant sum to set the place up, I think. Oh, and may I employ the Robinsons from your grandmother's house? They are not retirement age and they have both said they would like to work in the school. I originally thought we could manage with just myself and another teacher and a maid, but I think ... you see, the neighborhood ... I think we need a man."

Tommy burst out laughing. "*You*, Cecilia? You need a *man*? I never thought I should live to hear that from your lips. But of course, you may employ the Robinsons. It's a load off my mind, in fact. And draw from the bequest as soon as you like. Have the bills sent to me and I will see they are paid."

"But no!" exclaimed his wife. "No! That is precisely what I do not want. I want to manage my own affairs, if you please. Give the money to Mr. Davis, and I shall deal with it through him – if you don't mind," she added as an afterthought.

"I see," said Tommy. "As you wish, my dear. But may I at least see the premises where my wife will be spending her time?"

"Ye...es," replied Cecilia doubtfully. "But you will find it dreadfully dirty. You will spoil your coat. Perhaps you should wait until it is refurbished."

"As I've said before, Cecilia, while my coat is, of course, of great importance to me, it is not as important as you. If you can venture into this dirty, dangerous place, so can I. Coat be damned."

"Oh, Tommy, she said, coming and kneeling before him impetuously. "You really are the nicest man … I don't know how I have deserved such a good husband." She lifted his hand to her cheek.

Tommy smiled and put her hand to his lips. If only, he thought, he could show her what a good husband he wanted to be.

Chapter Sixteen

They said goodnight chastely later that night, Tommy disappearing into his room, and Cecilia into hers, next door, joined by communicating dressing rooms. Cecilia went thoughtfully to her bed, her mind on the visit to Chapel street the next morning, planning the work that needed to be done and trying to calculate the cost of it all. Tommy allowed Brooke to remove his coat and neckcloth, but since he was wearing no boots, dismissed him after that. He had not changed for dinner, since Cecilia had made no move to change from her wedding gown, other than to remove her veil. He slowly unbuttoned his waistcoat and shirt, then went to clean his teeth.

"You're a fool, my boy," he said to his reflection in the mirror. "All she cares for is her school. You are just a means unto that end. Get used to it."

He went to bed, but lay awake for a long time, staring at the ceiling as the flames of his fire died down into glowing coals and then disappeared altogether.

The following morning, Cecilia, who had slept quite well and had just left her bed, was surprised by a knock on the communicating door. She opened it to find Tommy smiling at her, clad in a gorgeous blue satin dressing gown, exactly the color of his eyes.

"Good morning!" he said. "May I come in?" He looked at her appreciatively. She was wearing a white cotton nightgown that reminded him of the ones his sister Mariah used to wear when she was a little girl. It was long-sleeved, with a broderie anglaise ruffle around the bottom and around the wrists. The neck was gathered and tied with a pink ribbon. She looked both virginal and absolutely desirable. He had to control himself not to take her in his arms.

"Of course," she said, oblivious to the effect she had on him. "What can I do for you?"

He swallowed. "Er ... well, nothing, really." He did not know where to begin. "Look, it's positively medieval, but ... well, we need to make it seem as if we ... we were together last night, so if you don't mind ..."

He did not finish the sentence, but went over to the bed, where he drew back the top covers, and, producing his razor from his pocket, made a small cut in the top of one of the fingers on his left hand, and smeared the blood on the bottom sheet. She gasped but quickly understood.

"It will save questions or conjecture," he said, then, kissing her hand, he went back the way he had come, calling over his shoulder, "I'll ring for hot water and for your fire to be made up."

Cecilia sat on the end of the bed, looking at the blood stain. Such a thing would never have occurred to her, but Tommy seemed to think of everything. Her thoughts went back to the reading of the Will, and the Dowager's words. What had she said? *In spite of the silliness we often observe in him but which I believe to be a complete affectation, he is a good boy and I trust him absolutely.* It was obvious to Cecilia that Tommy's grandmother had been nobody's fool. Like her, Cecilia was every day more convinced that his silliness was just an act. She wondered what he would have to say about her school premises; whatever it was, it would behove her to listen to him.

Tommy said nothing when they arrived in Chapel Street, though his eyebrows rose in surprise. He looked totally out of place in these filthy surroundings. He was still in mourning, of course, but his coat was cut to perfection and his boots gleamed. When he entered the dingy premises, he removed his hat and his gold head seemed to draw all the light into the place, and his bright blue eyes brought in the sky.

"Yes, I see," he said, after he had been all over the house. "You will use the one side for the school and the other side as a living space for the Robinsons and Bridget."

"And Lizzy," added Cecilia. She will be both pupil and cook. Mr. Davis says he has been able to obtain a very cheap lease on the place because of its condition, but I must say, I don't know where to begin with the repairs. I need reliable workers, and I know none, reliable or otherwise."

"Don't worry about that," replied Tommy. "We have estate carpenters, stonemasons, builders, painters, … and metal workers. We'll want bars on all the windows. That way, you can take the boards off and let the light in. We can put shelves and benches all around the schoolroom, like at John Pounds' place. I think it will be fine!"

He walked through into the scullery, frowned at the evidence of vermin, and then inspected the living quarters on the other side.

"I think it's best to tear out everything and build new," he declared finally. "Our people can do that. I'll have the estate agent decide whom we need, from Broome House or from Thyford. I daresay it won't take more than a month."

Cecilia listened to all this with growing astonishment and dismay. "But Tommy! You cannot make the estate people work for me! And what you are describing sounds enormously expensive. You know I can't afford it!"

Tommy took her hands, "My dear Cecilia! There is no *I* or *you* in this, there is only *we*. You are Lady Broome. If the estate workers cannot work for you, for whom can they work? And the only expense will be the materials they need. We already pay their wages. The Thyford group will enjoy a trip to London, I shouldn't wonder."

It took much persuasion before Cecilia was convinced, and at last she said, "Very well, since you think it best, but Tommy, you *must* tell me what this all costs over and above the wages because I *insist* on repaying the estate."

"As you wish, my dear, though heaven knows how I shall be able to work it out. All those columns of figures."

This was nonsense, as Tommy knew almost to a penny what the income and outgoings of his enormous estate were, but he had for so long denied all knowledge of it that, at times, he almost believed it himself. "Now, you are to come to Rothschild's with me. You have to decide which of the family jewels you would like to take out and have cleaned for wearing when you put off your black gloves." He put her hand on his arm and escorted her out of the building as if they were leaving the Palace.

Cecilia found herself swept along in some sort of dream. They went to the bank, where a bowing Director plied them with sherry and biscuits before introducing them into the vault. The Broome Deposit Box was opened and a casket extracted. Within were jewels that took Cecilia's breath away. She gingerly touched a necklace from a parure of sapphires.

"Great grandmother's sapphires," said Tommy. She had blue eyes, so my great grandfather bought her these. The settings are old fashioned, but the stones incomparable, don't you think? He was one of the few Allenbys with good taste."

He held them up to the light, and then put the tiara next to Cecilia's head. "Hmm. Not bad. You will look wonderful in any tiara, of course, but I wish they were emeralds rather than sapphires. Perhaps I should have one made for you ... emeralds with diamonds ..." his gaze wandered as he pictured it in his mind.

"No Tommy, please don't," said Cecilia urgently, "I cannot imagine I shall ever wear any tiara, and if I do, this one is perfect. It would remind me of you. You must have your great grandmother's eyes. They match yours, too."

"Well, if you think I'm going to wear it, you're way off, my girl," laughed Tommy. He opened other boxes until he found what he was looking for. "Ah, here they are, my mother's diamonds. We'll take these home. Once you're out of black gloves, these will look good with just about anything. Mother hardly ever wore them as she claimed her neck was too short. Actually, it was, really."

The diamonds in question were in the form of a necklace ending in a pendant, which, Tommy showed her, was actually detachable for wearing as a hair ornament. They were accompanied by a pair of earrings in the same design as the pendant.

"Your neck is most definitely not too short," considered Tommy, looking at her. "Here, let me screw on the earrings." His breath on her neck as he did so made Cecilia shiver, though not with cold. Then he nodded with satisfaction. "Lovely! They are made for you. Do you want to keep them on?"

"No, of course not. I can't wear diamonds now! I will take them if you want me to, but I can't imagine wearing them any time soon."

"I suppose not," agreed her husband. "Pity." He had to tamp down a desire to see her wearing nothing *but* the diamonds. He looked through a few more boxes, finally saying, "Well, at least these are emeralds," and holding up a huge square brooch made up of large emeralds and clusters of small pearls. "I can't imagine who this was made for. Looks like something from Good Queen Bess. Perhaps one of my forebears had it made for her in hopes of … well, something. It's far too large for any of the other women in the family, but on you it will be just right. I think we'll have an ivory silk gown made for you and you can wear this on one shoulder. Marvelous!"

She took it from his outstretched hand and looked at it. It was the largest piece of jewelry she had ever seen, and it was heavy. "If you say so, Tommy, but it will be rather like wearing a square bread-and-butter plate on my shoulder."

"As I said, marvelous!" confirmed her incorrigible husband, with a laugh. "Put it and the diamonds in your reticule and let's go home. I'm for lunch!"

And with a fortune in family jewels simply tucked into her reticule, Cecilia left the bank on the arm of her husband.

Chapter Seventeen

The next month passed in a whirl. What seemed like an army though which was in fact a select group of six workmen descended on the house in Chapel Street. Cecilia was adamant that the building be left as it was from the outside, as she did not want it so fine it would scare away would-be pupils. So, apart from replacing the broken roof tiles and taking down the the boards from the windows to replace them with iron bars stoutly cemented into the sills, it remained unchanged.

But from inside, sounds of hammering and sawing rose all day long. The leader of the group was the carpenter: an ox of a man with a broad chest and deep voice that effectively discouraged any nosy neighbors. On the day about two weeks into the renovations when Cecilia brought the Robinsons and Lizzy to see their new abode, she was amused to see this large fellow fall instantly under the young woman's spell. Good food and cheerful company had helped her regain her prettiness, and he helped her over the floors littered with blocks of wood, shavings, paint brushes and plaster much as a footman might help a queen.

Mr. Robinson's eyes brightened as he saw the back garden, rank and overgrown as it was. It had a northerly aspect, but since the building adjoining the main house was of one story only, it received some afternoon sun, which he declared would be enough to grow vegetables. Mrs. Robinson was horrified at the state of the privy, but vowed she would be back the next day with chloride of lime and a long handled scrubbing brush.

Once the roof was repaired and the chimneys were swept, the bedchambers were re-plastered, and the floors cleaned.

Fires were set in the grates to dispel the lingering damp. Downstairs, the kitchen furnishings, such as they were, had been completely removed, revealing a myriad of mouse and rat holes. Poison and plaster were applied. Then the giant young carpenter appeared one day with a skinny black and white cat.

"She don't look like much but they told me she was a good mouser. We'll see," he said.

When rows of dead mice began appearing as offerings in front of the kitchen hearth, they all agreed the problem seemed to have been solved.

A huge dresser with open shelves above and a cat cubby below was built along one wall, to hold plates and mugs. Cutlery was in the drawers beneath. Long tables ran on either side of a deep sink – the one original to the house, which, once cleaned, was found to be perfectly good. Underneath were ranged the buckets and pails for bringing in water from the pump.

As was customary, the kitchen was on the north side of the house and had a larder. This was essentially a thick-walled brick cupboard built out into the yard and exposed on three sides, with shelves made of stone. It was very cold in there now in the late autumn, and promised to remain cool all year. The large open hearth was cleaned and pots and pans hung from the hooks. A long table with several pine chairs was placed in the center of the room.

Lizzy inspected the kitchen and was in high excitement to move into the house. She and Bridget would occupy the bedchambers on the top floor, each with her own room for the first time in her life, and the Robinsons would take the second story.

In the schoolroom, shelves were hung and benches placed along the walls on two sides. A high wooden desk was constructed and placed on the third side next to a large piece of slate hung on the wall. Down the middle of the room ran a long deal table flanked by more benches.

As the renovations drew to an end, china, cutlery, mugs, linens, beds, cupboards and parlor furniture were supplied from the Dowager's house for the living quarters, not the fine French items that Mr. Robinson declared he would be afraid to sit on or burn with his pipe, but the comfortable and serviceable furnishings from the servants' quarters. Removed to Chapel Street, they were declared to be just the thing.

As Tommy had foretold, it was all ready in a month. The last piece to be finished was a long wooden plaque fixed above the school entrance bearing the carved and illuminated legend *Lady Ianthe Broome's School for Girls*. Mr. Robinson declared that the black and white cat, hitherto known only as The Cat, should be called Lady from then on.

When Tommy came to survey the renovated building, he smiled at the inscription. "I wonder what Grandmother would say if she saw that. I don't know that she ever thought very much about education for girls. She certainly thrust a number of very silly ones at me. And as for the cat, I never saw Gran with a large rat in her mouth, but I daresay if the occasion called for it, she would have been up to the task!"

He had sent a draft to Mr. Davis for the sum of his grandmother's legacy and dutifully billed him for building materials, as he had agreed with Cecilia. If Mr. Davis thought the bills strangely low, he said nothing to Cecilia, but was able to report to her that even having paid the first year's lease, the quarter's wages to the staff and the cost of the renovations, more than two-thirds of the legacy still remained. He was looking, he said, for an advantageous placement for the rest of the money.

The Robinsons, Lizzy and Bridget moved into the house and then began the process of encouraging local girls to come to the school. During the first few weeks, they would walk around the streets of the East End, telling any girl they saw that she could come that evening for lessons and a hot meal. Then they took to John Pounds' method, carrying hot potatoes in their pockets and promising more if they came to school.

Gradually, they came: first one or two, then girls with their sisters or their friends, girls carrying babies or bringing the toddlers they had to care for, girls in ragged dresses, girls with no shoes, girls with bruises, girls so thin they looked as if a puff of wind would blow them away, girls so tired they would fall asleep before the meal was served.

But they came; they listened to the stories Cecilia read from her story books, they watched her write the letters of the alphabet, and then words, on the wall slate, and one by one, tried to copy her. They clustered in groups around Bridget who showed them the words in the books and encouraged them to read, just as she had been encouraged. Some came only for the meal that was served after an hour and left early, but most stayed. At the end of six weeks, the school was up and running.

Mrs. Robinson dealt with ordering the food for the meals. She quickly established a reputation with the local shopkeepers as someone who could spot when a shopkeeper put his thumb on the scale to make the meat or vegetables weigh heavier, and would point out the cheat in a loud voice to everyone in the shop.

If girls were able to come in during the day, she taught them how to keep a household: how to wash, starch, iron and darn, how to clean. She taught them how to serve tea, how to be ready for work as a downstairs or upstairs maid.

Mr. Robinson hauled in the coal for the fires and started to clear the garden he would plant in the spring. In the evenings, he sat by the fire with his pipe in the front hall, often with babies or toddlers dozing on his lap, watching the door for rowdy lads who wanted to know what was going on. Some of them ended up sitting on the floor next to him and listening through the door to the stories and the lessons.

The giant young carpenter reappeared one day with the news that he had obtained a transfer from Thyford to Broome House. He claimed that a taste of London had given him a thirst for more, but everyone knew it was to see Lizzy. He became a regular in the evenings and began teaching some of the boys the elements of his trade, beginning with simple arithmetic, without which no carpenter can do his job. He worked with them on the kitchen table and pretended to be affronted when Lizzy smacked him out of the way.

At Broome House, Cecilia's life was altered in that instead of spending most of the day supervising the renovations in Chapel Street, she would now go there after luncheon and be home by eight in time to change for dinner with her husband.

Tommy had sent a simple notice to the newspapers to the effect that Cecilia Anne Beaumaris and Thomas Algernon Wymering Allenby, fourth Earl of Broome, had been married quietly in the presence of immediate family on the third of

November. As the family was still in mourning for the Dowager Duchess Ianthe, they would be receiving no guests and attending no social engagements for the foreseeable future. This meant that the couple dined quietly at home most evenings and went to only the smallest of gatherings.

Cecilia was usually so tired she usually went straight to bed when they returned home and was asleep almost immediately. It was otherwise with Tommy, who often went to his club when Cecilia went to bed, and if his friends were surprised to see a so recently married man amongst them, no one made any comment. In truth, he was finding his situation difficult to bear, but his intimates put his less than usually exuberant demeanor down to the loss of his grandmother, of whom he was known to be very fond.

Cecilia's birthday arrived and Tommy made as much fanfare of it as she let him. He would have liked a large family dinner, but after some discussion, they settled on an evening concert followed by a quiet supper tête à tête. At supper, she was astonished to receive from him a pair of emerald and pearl earrings, square like the broach, worn close to the earlobe.

"Had 'em made like that. Didn't think you'd want them dangling into your bread-and-butter plate" he laughed.

She impulsively took both his hands. "Oh, Tommy! Thank you," she said. "You keep giving me the most lovely things, and I give you nothing!" She blushed as she thought she did not even give him what any other husband might reasonably expect.

"Nonsense! You keep me endlessly entertained with stories from your school. I'm waiting with bated breath to see if our carpenter makes any real headway with young Lizzy, and to hear about the number of mice Lady the Cat laid at your feet yesterday, or how many babies Mr. Robinson had on his knee at one time. You've brought more into my life than you know, my dear."

Chapter Eighteen

Mr. Davis had sent Cecilia a note a few days earlier saying he would like to see her on a matter of importance. Accordingly, she invited him to Broome House the morning after her twenty-fifth birthday. She was now in full control of her own inheritance and the unspent bequest from the Dowager Duchess.

"As you know, my lady," said Mr. Davis, after looking around the drawing room at Broome House appreciatively, I have been investigating more … er remunerative placements for your capital. My father has had it invested in the Funds all these years, bringing in around three percent, as you know. But I believe we may do better."

He then went on to describe an investment opportunity in a Bolivian silver mine. A previously undiscovered large deposit had been reported a few months before. *The Times* had carried several columns about it. Perhaps her ladyship had seen it? She had not. The Anglo-Bolivian Mining Corporation, a mining exploration company, had been formed, with several well-known peers on the Board of Directors. Her ladyship had perhaps met Sir Felix Caversham? Or Lord Carstone? She had met them but could not say she knew them. In any case, early results of the exploration had been very encouraging and shares had been selling briskly. So far, the price had almost doubled. Mr. Davis would like to recommend she put a substantial sum into this investment. The way things were going, she would almost certainly make at least a fifty percent profit, and perhaps even double her money. But she needed to act fast, as the offering was to be closed.

Cecilia knew nothing about investments; indeed, she had no idea that an individual like herself could own part of a silver mine in a country so far away. But as she listened to Mr. Davis, she understood that this was how people became rich. If one did not, like Tommy, inherit land and enjoy the revenue from agriculture, one could make it through investment such as this. The idea that she could take her small fortune and double it was irresistible, not because she wanted anything for herself, but because then she would never have to worry that her school might run out of money. She told Mr. Davis to go ahead and acquire as many shares as he could.

Over dinner that night, she told Tommy what she had done. He looked at her seriously for a moment and then said,

"'Pon my word, Cecilia, I had no idea you were such a gambler. I would have hesitated to make such a move myself, but I daresay Mr. Davis is better informed than I."

"Oh yes, he seemed to be convinced that I would make a great deal more than just leaving my money in the Funds. I think it's so exciting!"

Her husband seemed on the point of saying something, but changed his mind and simply continued to eat his dinner.

Over the next couple of weeks, Cecilia found herself interested in the financial news, something she had never before even thought about. Tommy left the newspaper in the library when he had read it, usually quite late in the morning, for he breakfasted after a session at Gentleman Jack's Boxing establishment. This had been a surprise to Cecilia when she first discovered it, as he seemed the last person to engage in such a sport. With his obsessive attention to his clothing and his joking attitude, she could not envisage him in any form of fisticuffs. But she remembered that at the first ball they attended together, his friend had said he had a fierce left. In any case, after he had finished with it, Cecilia took to perusing the newspaper for any mention of the Anglo-Peruvian Mining Corporation. There was nothing.

One morning, she went into school early, before lunch, as Mrs. Robinson wanted to demonstrate the domestic skills of her maids-in-training. The housekeeper said she had had an idea, but first wanted her to imagine she was an employer examining the household linen, darned, washed, ironed, and in the case of the shirts, starched, by the girls. She should not be kind, but act exactly as a very demanding mistress would. This was hard for Cecilia, whose natural tendency was to excuse any shortcoming, but she did as she was asked and found the standard acceptable overall and, in some cases, very high.

Mrs. Robinson then suggested that this work could become a source of revenue for the girls: they would be paid for dealing with clients' linen during the day, and attend school at the end of it. The second downstairs room had been fitted out as a dining room, but it was virtually unused, since they all ate in the kitchen, so it could be used for drying when hanging outside was impossible.

Cecilia was glad to agree to anything that kept the girls off the streets and enabled them to safely provide income for their families. They had seen from the case of Lizzy that employment itself could sometimes be dangerous.

Having been at the school all day, Cecilia came home as dinner was being dished up, leaving a delighted Bridget in charge. She arrived back at Broome House more than an hour earlier than usual to find Tommy was still from home. She had not read the newspaper that morning, being in a hurry to leave, so she picked it up as she waited for Preston, the butler, to bring her in a cup of tea. She had no sooner opened it than to her horror she read headlines that made her heart stop.

Anglo-Bolivian Mine Hoax. Calls for Questions in the House.

Reports have arrived in London from a Mr. Peter Welliver, an engineer who travelled to Peru in the hopes of securing employment in the Anglo-Bolivian Mining Corporation. He has discovered that no such mine exists. He journeyed to Potosi, the given location of the above-mentioned Corporation and site of a number of mines, but discovered that none is owned by a company headquartered in London.

When this became known in the City yesterday afternoon, the share price dropped immediately, and it is expected that the slide will continue today. Attempts to reach the principals of the Corporation were fruitless: the offices on Fetter Lane appear to have been deserted. There are calls for Questions to be asked in Parliament.

Cecilia sank to her knees, her mouth open in a soundless "Oh", and then, as the full realization of what she had done hit her, a huge sob arose in her throat and tears began to course down her cheeks. She fell forward onto the carpet and sobbed. Preston came in with her tea.

"My lady, my lady, whatever can the matter be?" he cried, trying to raise her from the floor. "Come, sit up, please let me help you."

But she waved him off, unable to say anything but "No! No!"

At that moment a sound came from the hall outside and Preston ran out, to find Tommy standing, bemused, with no one to take his coat and hat.

"My lord!" cried the butler. "It's my lady! She's in a bad way. In the drawing room!" and he waved a flailing arm in that direction.

"What? She's home already? Goddammit! Why is she early, today of all days? I wanted to tell her …"

He threw his coat and hat to the floor and strode swiftly into the room to behold his wife, still on the carpet, crying as if her heart would break. Next to her, the scattered pages of the newspaper gave mute testament to what had caused the problem. Tommy shut the door in Preston's face and knelt beside his wife. He lifted her to a sitting position and drew her head onto his shoulder, where she wept uncontrollably.

"It's all right, my love, it's all right," he murmured into her hair. "You didn't lose your money. It's all right. You didn't lose it."

Cecilia gradually became aware of what he was saying and lifted her ravaged face. "What d…do y…you m…mean?" she hiccupped, trying to control her sobbing. "I…I don't un…understand."

"I suspected it was a bad investment. Anything that promises huge returns always is. I looked into it and became absolutely convinced it was a hoax. It wasn't the first, and it won't be the last. I'm … I'm afraid I used my husband's prerogative and told Davis to sell the stock two days after you bought it. He should have known better. In fact, his father came in while I was there and rang a peal over him for even suggesting it. The old man would never have done so. He was going to sell all their other holdings in the mine when I left them."

Cecilia looked at him, trying to take in what he was saying. "Y...you s...sold it?"

"Yes, I didn't dare tell you, as I knew you'd be angry with my interfering in your business. But I couldn't let you make that mistake. I'm sorry for being so high-handed, but it turns out to have been for the best."

"S...sorry? S...sorry?" cried Cecilia, laughing and crying at the same time. "Oh T...Tommy! Th...thank you! Thank you for being high ..." she hiccupped, "high-handed! Thank you for everything! I've been such a f...fool!"

Tommy stood up and helped her to her feet. He led her to the sofa and sat next to her. "You're not a fool. You were simply dealing in things you know nothing about. You need someone to help you, to look after you. That's me, you know. I'm your husband. It's my job. You can depend on me."

"Can I depend on you for a handkerchief again?" asked Cecilia, smiling and sniffing.

With a laugh, he put his hand in his pocket and gave it to her. She wiped her eyes and blew her nose and tried to tuck up her hair, which was falling from its pins.

"I must look a sight!" she said ruefully. Then she gave a watery smile. "Oh, Tommy, what have I done to deserve a husband like you? You are kind, thoughtful, generous ... and all I've done is cause you trouble. You must rue the day you met me!"

Tommy grasped both her hands. "The day I met you was the best day of my life!" he said, then took a deep breath, "Cecilia, I love you. I've loved you since I made you cry at Lady March's dining table. I loved you when I persuaded you to become betrothed. I loved you when I persuaded you to accept the terms of Gran's legacy and marry me. I think, with time, I can persuade you to love me, too. Will it help if I tell you that you did actually make money on your investment? The price had gone up by the time I sold it."

He was silent for a moment, then spoke, as if having made up his mind. "But since it's the time for confessions, I should tell you that though I bless her for making marriage a condition of her bequest, as for the legacy itself, it was a lovely idea, but that's all it was – an idea. She had spent her fortune ages ago and had nothing to leave. Unlike you, she had no idea of thrift and the estate had been paying her bills for years. I gave Davis the money myself when you said you wanted to handle it. I'm sorry, I should have told you."

Cecilia listened to all this, hardly believing her ears. Then she burst into tears again.

"My love!" cried Tommy, gathering her to him, "What have I said? I didn't mean any of it, if it's going to make you cry!"

Her eyes streaming with tears, but feeling as if a huge weight had been lifted from her shoulders, Cecilia sobbed, "But T...Tommy! I d...do love you! I j...just didn't w...want t...to admit it." She gulped and made a huge effort. "I...I was used to being different and a...alone. I c...couldn't understand why you were so kind to me. I thought you were sorry for me, a...and I didn't want to g...get too close. But I do love you. I d...do." She caught her breath again and at last got herself under control. "Oh dear," she said, "and now I've ruined your c...coat. It's all wet."

"To hell with the coat," said Tommy sternly. "How many times have I told you that you are more important than my damned coat?" He took hold of her and kissed her fiercely. Cecilia held back at first, but then melted into his arms. It felt wonderful to just give in.

"Look here, Cecilia," he said when he finally let her go, "I don't want to take advantage of you in your weakened state, but if I love you and you love me, and we're man and wife, what are we doing sitting here? Don't you think there's a better way to show it? Come on. Let's go upstairs and make it official."

Cecilia blushed and caught her breath, but did not hesitate. She rose and followed him willingly to the door.

As they walked arm in arm swiftly towards the stairs, Tommy turned to Preston, who was, as usual hovering in the hall.

"Tell Cook," he said, "that dinner will be delayed ... for some time."

"Certainly, my lord," bowed the Butler with a smile.

The End

A Note From the Author

Thank you for reading my second novel, **Cecilia or Too Tall to Love**. If you enjoyed it, **please leave a review on the book's Amazon page** (link and QR code below) Amazon ranks authors by their reviews and it would help me very much! Thank you!

https://www.amazon.com/Cecilia-Too-Tall-Love-Regency/dp/B084DGQDW5/ref=

As a 6ft. tall woman who was for many years a teacher, this is a story near to my heart! Fortunately, I discovered I wasn't Too Tall To Love! If you look on my website, you'll see pictures of my grandchildren! You can also sign up for a FREE SHORT STORY!

https://romancenovelsbyglrobinson.com

Regency Novels by GL Robinson

Imogen or Love and Money Lovely young widow Imogen is pursued by Lord Ivo, a well-known rake. She angrily rejects him and concentrates on continuing her late husband's business enterprises. But will she find that money is more important than love?

Cecilia or Too Tall to Love Orphaned Cecilia, too tall and too outspoken for acceptance by the *ton,* is determined to open a school for girls in London's East End slums, but is lacking funds. When Lord Tommy Allenby offers her a way out, will she get more than she bargained for?

Rosemary or Too Clever to Love Governess Rosemary is forced to move with her pupil, the romantically-minded Marianne, to live with the girl's guardian, a strict gentleman with old fashioned ideas about young women should behave. Can she save the one from her own folly and persuade the other that she isn't just a not-so-pretty face?

The Earl and The Mud-Covered Maiden The House of Hale Book One. When a handsome stranger covers her in mud driving too fast and then lies about his name, little does Sophy know her world is about to change for ever.

The Earl and His Lady The House of Hale Book Two. Sophy and Lysander are married, but she is unused to London society and he's very proud of his family name. It's a rocky beginning for both of them.

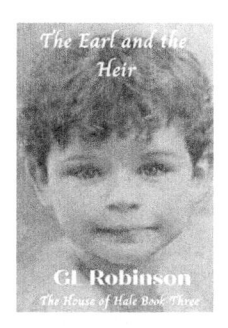

The Earl and The Heir The House of Hale Book Three. The Hale family has a new heir, in the shape of Sylvester, a handful of a little boy with a lively curiosity. His mother is curious too, about her husband's past. They both get themselves in a lot of trouble.

The Kissing Ball A collection of Regency short stories, not just for Christmas. All sorts of seasons and reasons!

The Lord and the Red-Headed Hornet Orphaned Amelia talks her way into a man's job as secretary to a member of the aristocracy. She's looking for a post in the Diplomatic Service for her twin brother. But he wants to join the army. And her boss goes missing on the day he is supposed to show up for a wager. Can feisty Amelia save them both?

The Lord and the Cat's Meow A love tangle between a Lord, a retired Colonel, a lovely debutante and a fierce animal rights activist. But Horace the cat knows what he wants. He sorts it out.

Book Group Conversation Starters

I love Book Groups and belong to four! Below, you'll find some Book Group Conversation Starters. I hope you have fun with them!

1. Cecilia thinks she is too tall to love. Do you think such an idea might enter a young woman's mind today? Do you think body image considerations affect young women more or less than in the past?

2. In spite of his frivolous appearance and demeanor, Tommy is obviously a deep-thinking person. Do you think young men today are encouraged to show their true feelings, or cover them up? Do you think young men today face more or fewer challenges in personal relationships than in the past?

3. Tommy's grandmother is constantly trying to arrange a marriage for him. What do you think of parents or grandparents trying to introduce suitable partners to their sons and daughters? What do you think of arranged marriages?

4. Cecilia was besieged by fortune hunters. Do people still marry for money?

5. Romance novels with happy endings are immensely popular. They are amongst the best-selling genres on Amazon. Why?

Printed in Great Britain
by Amazon